F...

My dogs over the ye[ars have been more] than family. So I dedicate this book to them and the Service Dogs around the world who sacrifice to help mankind in our darkest hours for little reward asked for.

First Published 2019 Great Britain

Copyright (C) 2019 Stuart Kevin Manley

All rights reserved. No part of this publication may be reproduced, stored in a retrieval system, or transmitted in any form or by any means, electronic, mechanical, photocopying, recording or otherwise, without prior permission from the copyright owners.

CASE FILE:- The New Guard

Content

Chapter one: Bad news.   Page 4

Chapter two: Trumpton town camp.   Page 14

Chapter three: Medical and Physical.   Page 21

Chapter four: Basic training.   Page 44

Chapter five: New beginnings.   Page 66

Chapter six: Secrets revealed   Page 110

Chapter seven: Time waits for no one!
                                          Page 126

Chapter eight: Never trust a German
               sausage!   Page 140

Chapter nine: The tale of two tunnels.
                                          Page 148

CASE FILE:- The New Guard

Chapter ten: The German HQ, end of the line?

Page 169

Chapter eleven: Weakness's can be our greatest strengths   Page 199

Chapter twelve: Freedom is not at any cost.

Page 231

Chapter Thirteen: You can always find success from failure.   Page 256

Maps

Map of Europe 1915.   Page 270

Map of Mission Objectives.   Page 271

CASE FILE:- The New Guard

TOP SECRET

Ministry Of Canine Defence

CASE FILE:- The New Guard

The Watch Dog Division.

Chapter 1... Bad news.

It is the year 1914 at a secret location on the edge of quiet village in Bedfordshire England. The war has left an eerie silence in the neighbourhood as the men young and old have been called up to do their duty leaving behind the women, also not forgetting our four legged friends to do their part to.

Two such four legged friends was Captain Poopstacker known to his master and friends as Bentley. Bentley was young to be an officer, but

CASE FILE:- The New Guard

Captain Bentley Poopstacker.

Special Dog Squadron - Watch Dog Division Operative

Serial number: 247592

Gender: Male

Breed: Olde English Bulldogge

Age: 19 Months

due to his heroism or stupidity during a stint in latrine duty he single handily saved the camp from a methane explosion so was awarded the brown star for his actions and a commission to be an officer. From that point on he became the Special Dog Squadrons head in explosives and sabotage. Beside him and listening intently was Major Dude who was

CASE FILE:- The New Guard

very different to Captain Poopstacker, unlike Captain Poopstackers Bulldog looks and lack of charm Major Dutch Dude was a charismatic dog small black and tan from the North of England with rakish wiry good looks and an eye for trouble.

Major Dutch Dude

Special Dog Squadron - Watch Dog Division Operative

Serial number: 247591

Gender: Male

Breed: Lakeland terrier

Age: 7 years

Captain Poopstacker reports to the Major in his rough deep voice "Major there's trouble a foot, have

CASE FILE:- The New Guard

you heard the news?" "Yes" replied the Major. "I have heard the news, we will certainly have to step up are training over the next few weeks, if we have any chance to be picked to go to the front!"

Now the Major and the Captain before the war had been at home with their Master Kevin. Kevin who was a middle-aged man lived out in the countryside together for the last few years and then one day a letter arrived at the door. Master Kevin's face dropped he had been ordered to war, Kevin knew he had to do his duty, but was panic stricken by the thought of having to leave his two four legged friends behind. He quickly arranged with some old

CASE FILE:- The New Guard

friends for the two dogs to be kept together until he came back from the war.

The day came when he dropped them off and had to say goodbye. He bent down stroking the pair of them and nestled his head in to theirs as he was trying to hold back the tears as he said "don't worry lads, you be good boys and I'll see you soon. No matter what, look after each other." Both dogs knew something was up and started to plead for Kevin not to go. Kevin had no choice and had turned slowly on his heels then walked off down the garden path heading off to war with tears rolling down his face at the thought he may not see the two of them again. Immediately after Kevin had gone

CASE FILE:- The New Guard

Dutch and Bentley set to work to try and find away to reunite with their master. A few days past and Dutch had heard on the Canine hotline, a collie six doors down that the Army were recruiting Dogs to go to war. "That's it Bentley, we can join up and find Kevin!" Dutch announced. Bentley on the other hand had started to get use to his new home, with two good meals and the settee to lounge on plus listening to the gramophone. "Really?" said Bentley "It's nice here and I'm just settling in." Dutch because of age and superiority within the pack looked at Bentley then with a growl in his voice "Bentley for once in your life you will do what's right and not whatever you please!! Bentley looked sheepish and immediately took back

CASE FILE:- The New Guard

what he had said then apologised to Dutch. "I'm sorry Dutch, but what chance do we have of joining the Army in the first place? They're looking for dogs like Airedales and Bull mastiffs! Just look at us. You're a small Lakeland terrier who's middle-aged and I'm young Bulldogge with an over active bowel!! So as I say, what chance have we got?" Dutch looked at him up and down, "you're right Bentley we have little chance, but we have to try, if we don't we will regret this decision for the rest of our days!"

So early the next morning they packed their small belongings between them and preceded on with their

CASE FILE:- The New Guard

plan, but little that they knew it would change their lives forever.

5.30 am Bentley runs up to the old couple's bedroom who were looking after them and checks they are both snoring away blissfully, unaware what is unfolding down stairs.....

Dutch is on the window seat at the front of the house and eases the window latch open and with a gentle push the window opens. "Bentley!" he whispers, Bentley then as agile as Bulldog can be quietly sneaks down the stairs to where Dutch is waiting. Bentley whispers to Dutch, "Dutch are you sure about this?" "Yes I'm sure! Now hurry before

CASE FILE:- The New Guard

they wake up!" Bentley goes first by trying to climb on to the window seat, but due to his lack of agility is struggling. "Don't panic, look stand on me" says Dutch. As soon as he had said it he immediately regretted his decision. "Bentley, will you move? I can't breathe!" Bentley pulled himself up on to the window seat and looked down at Dutch who was now trying to retrieve his breath. Bentley knew the best thing was to just go out through the window and wait for Dutch to calm down.

A few moments later they were both out in the garden looking at each other. Bentley sheepishly apologises to Dutch, Dutch turns to Bentley and tells him not to worry. "So where are we going?"

CASE FILE:- The New Guard

asks Bentley. "There's a recruiting training camp just outside Trumpton town, let's get going its 10 miles and we're hopefully be there for lunch time." Dutch replies. "Lunch time? Come on let's get going" Bentley replies excitedly, thinking about lunch. "You and your stomach Bentley" says Dutch as he shakes his head.

Meanwhile at the old couple's cottage the couple have awoken to find the dogs missing, to all in purpose to them it looked like to them that the dogs had been stolen! So in obvious distress had contacted the local police to file a report of their disappearance.

CASE FILE:- The New Guard

Chapter 2... Trumpton Town Camp

The two dogs looked up at the poster outside the camps gates. The poster had a picture of an Airedale terrier standing proud with the slogan "Your Country Needs You, recruit today!"

"See I told you it was true, they do need us." says Dutch... "Okay, Okay, I believe you!" says Bentley trying not to lose too much face.

"Okay. What do you two want then?" the two dogs turned and guarding the gates is a Bull Mastiff on sentry duty, rippling with muscles and a scar across his face. "We are here to sign up." says

CASE FILE:- The New Guard

Dutch in his most dignified voice. "Really?" says

Sergeant Leo Manley.
Regimental Police
Serial number: 241692
Gender: Male
Breed: Bull Mastiff
Age: 6 years

the Bull Mastiff in a sarcastic tone, "the both of you?" By this stage Bentley was having second thoughts and was now thinking of the that lovely settee and treats he had left behind. "Yes both of us!" Dutch replied more forcefully this time, in which both took the sentry by surprise

CASE FILE:- The New Guard

and snapped Bentley out of his day dream. "Okay you two follow me" replied the sentry. The two of them followed the sentry through the gates and as they looked about they noticed an Old English sheepdog walking towards them, he was grey in the muzzle but still had a spark of life in his eye, he called to the sentry "Sergeant who are these fellows and what are they doing here?" The sentry replied by coming to attention, saluting and replied with a smirk" Captain, Sir these gents have come to enlist and win the war for us..." as he looked at our unlikely heroes up and down. " That's enough out of you thank you sergeant, you two gents please follow me." said the Captain. Bentley and Dutch followed

CASE FILE:- The New Guard

the Captain to a nearby office in which the Captain invited them to enter. "Come in and sit down the two of you and tell me about yourselves and why you wish to enlist?" Our heroes proceed to tell the Captain about themselves and why they want to join. "Okay gents we need to do a physical and a background check before you can go any further though" the Captain warned them; Bentley is now looking extremely worried at the thought of a physical examination! Out of the Captain sight Dutch laid his paw on Bentleys paw as to comfort and reassure him not to worry. Dutch at the same time chirps up and asks the question "a background check, what's that for?" The Captain looked at him from across the desk and replied "well we don't

CASE FILE:- The New Guard

know whether or not you have escaped from a dog pound or if there are any outstanding police warrants do we?" "I mean we couldn't have common criminals here, you wouldn't know who you could trust." Dutch nodded in agreement with the Captain and proceeded to leave with Bentley out of the office then waited outside for the Captain to do his enquires with the local authorities.

A short time later the Captain appeared at the door and then beckoned them back into the office to carry on their interview. The Captain turned to Dutch and Bentley then started to grill the pair of them, " okay the pair of you what can you tell me about this police file?" Dutch and Bentley are

CASE FILE:- The New Guard

shocked by this result and puzzled? " I don't understand Sir?" says Dutch, the captain barked back at him " well the police are certainly looking for you two though. So can you shed some light on this matter?" Dutch and Bentley looked at each other quizzically, for all their might they could not think why the police were looking for them? They had always stayed on the right side of the law? The Captain relaxed his gaze, smiled and reassured them " try to take those worried looks off of your faces I'm just having some fun with you, the Police are looking for you as they think you've been stolen. So please enlighten me on the matter?" As he laughed at the matter, the pair explained what must have happened then in an

CASE FILE:- The New Guard

instant the Captain made his decision "right lets clear this mess up shall we. I shall contact the couple you were staying with, I'll reassure them that you're safe and under the protection of the Army now. I'll also inform the Police to drop the matter and that will be that. Okay?"

"Yes Captain and thank you very much Sir" replied Dutch and Bentley with relief. "Oh don't thank me yet gents, you have no idea what's ahead of you!"

CASE FILE:- The New Guard

Chapter 3.... Medical and physical!

The Captain handed our two heroes over to a Corporal Nailer, a tall handsome Airedale terrier who had a spring his step and a kind but firm attitude. "Come on you two, you've got some tests to do before you can start your training, so follow me," the Corporal ordered.

Corporal Max Nailer.
Infantry
Serial number : 247100
Gender : Male
Breed : Airedale Terrier
Age : 5 years

CASE FILE:- The New Guard

The three of them headed over to the Physical and Medical centre. Once through the doors Bentley gulped at what awaited for them. "I don't like the look of this Dutch!" Bentley whispered, "sshh, it'll be Okay, don't worry I'm with you," replied Dutch, quietly trying desperately to reassure Bentley. They approached the first cubicle a Doctor asked for their details, and then proceeded to take blood and then off to the next cubicle for an eye test and hearing. "See nothing to worry about" said Dutch, "I suppose you're right" replied Bentley. Then off to the next cubicle weight and height! The two dogs looked at each other and wondered how they were going to get away with this one? They

CASE FILE:- The New Guard

entered the room, a Nurse asked Bentley to stand on the scales, Bentley looked sheepish, he knew that he was a bit chubby, he always said it was puppy fat and nothing to do with all the biscuits and treats he ate most of the time. He's ethos is might go to waste and it tastes so good. The scales swept around and hovered at 30kg, "Oops, there must be something wrong with your scales!" Bentley sheepishly said. "That's funny they were only calibrated yesterday?" replied the nurse "let me check "said the nurse, "off you get." Bentley stepped off the scales and the nurse stepped on, Bentley was now willing the needle around, Please be heavier, please! He thought to himself. The scales needle came stationary at 22kg, Bentley's

CASE FILE:- The New Guard

shoulders dropped in disappointment. "Don't worry, with a strict diet and exercise we'll soon have you in to shape" the nurse said cheerfully. Bentley on the other hand on hearing diet and exercise had just died a little bit inside and was trying his best to hold back the tears.

Dutch went through the weigh in with no problems 15kg, maybe a bit light for soldier but no problem, so on to height.

The height bar was brought down on to Bentley 20 inches with no problems, now on to Dutch. Now Dutch being a typical terrier was short in structure but not in courage, that was not going to help him now. He looked to Bentley to distract the

CASE FILE:- The New Guard

nurse, in which he did in glorious fashion by pretending to faint due to a lack of food. The nurse quickly came to Bentley's aid whilst Dutch proceeded to stack some metal dog bowls under the measuring platform. He glanced around and realised he hadn't been seen and proceeded to hop up on to the platform. " Nurse, Nurse I'm sure he'll be okay, I'm ready to proceed when you are?" said Dutch the poor nurse was stuck between dealing with Bentley and Dutch so replied " please could you just lower the measuring bar down until it's touching you." "No problem my dear, it is done!" The nurse glanced around and Dutch's measurement was 19.5 inches? She glanced again in disbelief but had to come to terms with the result as she sat there

CASE FILE:- The New Guard

puzzled. "Oh I'm going again!" said Bentley, as he winked at Dutch, in which gave enough time for Dutch to slide the bowls out and reset the measuring device back to normal. Dutch then rushed over to Bentley then proceeded to gently slap him on the side of face and said "pull yourself together. We'll going to the canteen right this instant." As soon as the word canteen had exited Dutch's mouth Bentley was up on his feet and through the door. "My apologises for him" said Dutch to the nurse" he has no manners." he then followed Bentley out of the door were they met up outside. "Okay where's the canteen?" asked Bentley. "Will you give it a break, it's always food with you!" replied Dutch. "But I'm hungry! I haven't

CASE FILE:- The New Guard

eaten for at least 2 hours!" as Bentley stood there sulking. Dutch knew from previous experience it is never good to upset a moody Bulldogge. "Ok well let's find the corporal and he can take us to the canteen. After a short walk around the base with Bentley grumbling in tow they finally meet up with the corporal they had met earlier, Corporal Nailer. "All done then lads at the medical?" the corporal asked. "Yes Corporal" replied Dutch. "And the physical?" The corporal questioned. "Physical? I thought that's what we had just done?" Dutch replied." No, you still have the physical fitness to complete yet!" the corporal informed them with a grin. "What? No! I'm too weak with hunger!" Bentley gasped in reply. The Corporal looked at them, then to his watch. "Hmm Okay it's

CASE FILE:- The New Guard

near enough to lunch, come with me" he commands the two of them.

Bentley's spirits arose; finally he will be able to satisfy his hunger pains.

The canteen was a well organised place and the military cooks had laid out plenty of locally produced, freshly cooked food for the camp. Bentley's eyes glazed over with the amount of food that was on offer. Dutch stood there staring at Bentley in shock as he watched Bentleys eyes glaze over with what was now looking like white shoe laces of drool hanging from the corners of his mouth! "Bentley! Bentley NO!" cried Dutch as he could envision the carnage that Bentley was going

CASE FILE:- The New Guard

to do to the canteen. Dutch was busily trying to get in front of Bentley to stop him from making a pig of himself. Suddenly this huge figure appeared from the corner of Dutch's vision, who proceeded to push in between the pair of them. Bentley stopped in his tracks and looked up. There in front of him seemed a mountain of dog with a head as big as Dutch's whole body!

"Right, you little urchin, I'm Sergeant Major Flynn and who are you?" he asked as the Sergeant Major bent his gigantic head down looking poor Bentley in the eye. "Gulp! I'm Bentley Sir." replied Bentley. "Sir, Sir, I'm not an officer I work for a living lad!" as he barked at Bentley in his strong Irish accent." You will address me as Sergeant Major Flynn in the future. Understand?" "Yes Sergeant

CASE FILE:- The New Guard

Major." Bentley stuttered out in response, feeling sorry for himself. At this stage Corporal Nailer came forward then addresses the Sergeant Major on who these two unlikely heroes are. Dutch at this time was in awe of the Sergeant Major, he had heard of the giant Irish dogs that in the past who had fought wolves to defend mankind but up until this day he had never laid eyes on one.

After his conversation with the Corporal the Sergeant Major made his departure from the canteen with one final comment to Bentley on the way out "I'm watching you my lad!" he had said, Bentley had felt his whole body go numb in response.

CASE FILE:- The New Guard

Regimental Sergeant Major Patrick Flynn.

Infantry

Serial number: 246009

Gender: Male

Breed: Irish wolfhound

Age: 9 years

It may well of been the gentle prep talk that Bentley had received from the Sergeant Major, but for some reason he had lost his appetite slightly. After a refreshing lunch plus a very quiet Bentley who was still thinking about the Sergeant Major plus what was going to happen next? They were now back for their physical fitness test.

CASE FILE:- The New Guard

The two of them plus the Corporal had proceeded to the back of the medical centre to what was now in front of them. There were walls, ropes, holes, barbed wire, mud, lots of mud! Great! Thought Dutch, Bentley had turned as white as a sheet at the thought. "But I'm still weak" Bentley moaned annoyingly" "Shut up Bentley, it will be fun." replied Dutch. " OK lads are you listening? The course is timed and you have to beat 12 minutes to pass, Ok?" the Corporal explained. "Yes Corporal" Dutch acknowledged Bentley just nods yes as he really wasn't listening; he was still shocked at the sight that laid out in front of him. Exercise me! He thought. They lined up at the starting point and the Corporal indicated to go, and then started the

CASE FILE:- The New Guard

stop watch. They're off! Dutch goes off like a hare with Bentley was trying his best to keep up. "Wait for me!" Bentley pleads with Dutch.

Whilst the pair was off trying their best on the assault course the Corporal is intensely watching them and he hadn't noticed a small but powerful figure siding up to him. "Afternoon Corporal" the figure announced. The Corporal jumped more in surprise than anything else, and then turned to where this voice had come from, he looked down and there standing at the side of him was a small, old, red Lakeland terrier with a monocle and flying cap on. "Can I help you?" the Corporal enquired. Before

CASE FILE:- The New Guard

he could say anything the small red Lakeland introduced himself as Brigadier Baggins, to verify his rank and position he showed his identification warrant.

"My apologies Sir, how can I help you?" The Corporal replied as he brought himself to attention and saluted the Brigadier." "Those two running the assault course have you their files on you?" the

CASE FILE:- The New Guard

Brigadier enquired. The Corporal replied quizzically "No sir, their back in the office." "Hmm, be a good fellow and fetch them for me please." ordered the Brigadier. "But sir, I wouldn't waste your time on these two!" replied the Corporal. "I'll be judge of that Corporal" as the Brigadier pressed his point. "Yes Sir" the Corporal answered and off he rushed to fetch the two files.

The Brigadier stood and watched the two running the assault course like an eagle looking for small signs, that these two might be what he was looking for? Dutch was having a whale of a time climbing and diving through holes, Bentley on the other hand was not, he was struggling. Dutch had already

CASE FILE:- The New Guard

turned around and helped Bentley over the obstacles and for his troubles he had Bentley whinging about how much he hated the mud and everything to do with exercise. Dutch gritted his teeth and kept on encouraging Bentley even though it was hard at times.

"Sir here are the files you asked for." the Corporal informed the Brigadier as he tried to compose himself after running from one end of the camp to the other. "Thank you. I hope it wasn't too much trouble?" the Brigadier replied with an impish smile. The Brigadier took the files and started to scan through them.

CASE FILE:- The New Guard

"Well that's it their past the 12 minute mark they've failed!" the Corporal announced. The Brigadier didn't reply he just watched the two entering the last part of the assault course. It was the wall and poor Bentley had tried his hardest he was a few inches away from reaching the top. Dutch looked at him as Bentley kept scrabbling at the wall. "We're not going to fail Bentley." he informed him. "But I can't do it!" Bentley replied looking sorry for himself. "Bentley we're brothers, I'm not going to leave you behind, stand on me." Dutch gently replied. Dutch proceeded to crouch down in front of the wall and Bentley climbed on Dutch he then was able to grab the top of the wall then pulled himself up. "I've done it!" cried Bentley

CASE FILE:- The New Guard

with delight. "Great, now give me your paw and pull me up" Dutch answered. That was it they were over the last hurdle and across the finishing line. As they stood therepanting and trying to catch their breath they suddenly realised the Corporal wasn't alone.

The Brigadier was the first to speak "Well done you two." "Thank you Sir." Dutch replied, Bentley just waved an acknowledgment as he was still trying to find his breathe. Corporal Nailer broke up their congratulations "Sorry lads, 13 minutes on the test and you know what that means." Dutch's heart dropped as he looked at Bentley as he knew that the time could've been better, but Bentley was his

CASE FILE:- The New Guard

little brother, time or not they completed it together. "Well it's a good job I have the final say on such matters isn't it Corporal?" The Brigadier chirped up, The Corporal looked stunned and couldn't help himself questioning the Brigadiers decision. The Brigadier turned and spoke to Dutch and Bentley "My lads you are what I'm looking for, not once did you give up when things got tough and you always helped each other to succeed in your tasks. Don't worry about the time; with the right training we'll soon have you fighting fit." "Right Corporal, I leave them in your capable hands for basic training and inform me when they're ready." The Brigadier ordered and then turned on his heels and made his exit.

CASE FILE:- The New Guard

Oh great! Thought the Corporal, "OK you two come with me to the barracks as it looks like you're staying." he announced to the two of them. Great thought Dutch we're in, Bentley was thinking of a nice bed to recover from his ordeal.

CASE FILE:- The New Guard

Chapter 4.... Basic Training.

Basic training as you can guess was not going to be easy for our budding heroes, but remembering the speech from the Brigadier they persevered. Over the weeks both them started to notice a difference in themselves, they became stronger, more focused than they ever had been. They had found self confidence.

It was now week 5 and the two of them were heading over to the gymnasium as they were just about to enter the building a young beautiful English Bull terrier was waiting for them at the door. "Morning privates, you're with me today." she informed them. Dutch's heart skipped a beat as he

CASE FILE:- The New Guard

stumbled to reply "Oh yes Mam!" "Private. I am Sergeant Rosa Cribb." the Sergeant corrected him. They followed her in to the gym where she properly introduced herself and that she had been ordered to the camp to teach the pair of them unarmed combat and martial arts by the Brigadier.

"Right privates, I'm going to teach over the coming weeks the martial arts of Shi-tsu and Barkido with these skills it will help you to keep yourselves alive!" the Sergeant announced. Dutch thought great he was going to get the chance to be close to her and then he would use his charm to hopefully ask her out that evening.

CASE FILE:- The New Guard

Bentley's thoughts were not in the same camp, no not at all, all he could think was that no female would be able to beat him in a fight, as he chuckled to himself. Bentley was the first to step forward and volunteer to attack the young Sergeant on the mats.

Sergeant Rosa Cribb

Special Dog Squadron Operative

PT instructor and Combat instructor

Serial number: 2472100

Gender: Female

Breed: English Bull Terrier

Age: 6 years

CASE FILE:- The New Guard

Sergeant Rosa stood composed and waited for Bentley to attack. "Go ahead" she ordered. Bentley rushed her attempting to push her over so he could pin her down. The last thing Bentley knew that one minute he was upright and the next he was flying through the air head first on to the mats! He hit the mats like a sack of spuds. Winded but still willing to go on, he stood up "Again!" ordered the Sergeant. This time Bentley took it slower; his plan was to get in close then bear hug her until she submitted. He grabbed her with both paws, but at that instance she squatted down then with her paws together forced them between his and broke his grip. Before he could think, she stepped forward and swept his legs from under him to which

CASE FILE:- The New Guard

Bentley crashed to the mat, then which to add to insult the Sergeant pinned him down then started to twist his ears until he submitted. Dutch was struggling at this point to retain from laughing at Bentleys expense. Bentley on the other hand had limped off the mat to nurse his injured pride then sat down. "Come on Private Dude, your next" Sergeant Rosa ordered. Dutch sprung to his feet then casually walked over to the Sergeant and stood in front of her. Dutch proceeded then to attempt to ask the Sergeant out on a date that evening, in which she was very flattered then as a gesture Dutch took her paw to kiss it, the next thing Dutch knew is that he had been swung up off of the floor, swung around her shoulders and was now flying

CASE FILE:- The New Guard

through the air towards Bentley, who was now laughing uncontrollably at the sight of Dutch, that was until Dutch hit him in the chest head first. "Okay you two have a rest and I'll show you on the chalk board where you were going wrong" Sergeant Rosa spoke in her calm voice.

After some time that afternoon the two lads had started to understand the basics. They were proceeding to leave for the day when the Sergeant pulled Dutch to one side and asked him where he was taking her that evening? "I was thinking an evening at the theatre?" Dutch replied nervously. "Yes that will be great, pick me up at 7.00pm and don't be late!" Rosa answered. "OK, see you then."

CASE FILE:- The New Guard

Dutch answered. "Great you have a date, what am I suppose to do this evening?" Bentley asked Dutch. "Give me a few minutes and I'll work something out for you." Dutch replied as he raced off.

A short while later Dutch catches up with Bentley, "Right, I've sorted your evening for you." Dutch tells Bentley with a grin on his face. "Okay what am I doing?" replied Bentley. Dutch proceeds to tell Bentley that he had, had a word with the Camp cooks at the canteen and asked whether or not they needed a hand to clear up after the evening meal, the answer was yes. Dutch explained it to Bentley who looked at him quizzically "But that means I have to work!?" Bentley questioned. "No think

CASE FILE:- The New Guard

about it, all the left over's that are thrown in the bin!" Dutch answers. "Oh! Oh yes!" Bentleys replied as his eyes started to enlarge at the thought of all that food. Bentley couldn't control himself as he danced about like a puppy "thank you, thank, you" he kept telling Dutch. "No problem, I just hope you enjoy your evening and I'll see you later" Dutch replied.

The evening went well for them both, but this was the Army and not a vacation so they quickly had to knuckle down again and carry on with their training the next morning.

"Morning, how did your evening go Bentley?" asked Dutch as he gazed towards Bentleys bloated

CASE FILE:- The New Guard

stomach! "It was great, not one scrap wasted." replied Bentley with a grin. "Oh no I feel sorry for the ones cleaning the latrines today!" laughed Dutch.

So off they went for weapon training, after a short walk they were met at the entrance to the firing range by a tall Scottish deerhound "Good morning to you, I'm Corporal Hamish and I will be you're instructor for the day, follow me." The two of them followed the Corporal to the firing position in which to one side was an arrangement of firearms laid out on a table with boxes of ammunition beside it.

CASE FILE:- The New Guard

Both Dutch and Bentley's eyes lit up at the site of the guns and couldn't wait to have a go. The Corporal eyed them up and down and then proceeded to ask "who has actually fired a gun?" The two both replied that they had never seen a gun let alone fired one. "Okay well we will start at the beginning with gun safety and once I'm happy that you're safe we will take it to the next level." the Corporal responded.

After what seems to be ages to both Dutch and Bentley the Corporal was finally happy with their gun safety so were now ready to fire the guns. "Ok what would you like to try first?" The Corporal asked. Bentley was the first to answer excitedly "I

CASE FILE:- The New Guard

want a go of the Machine gun. Please!" Dutch answered "May I use the rifle please." "Yes no problem lads, right make sure the guns are safe, bolts back, check the breach as you pick them up, well done. Remember never point the gun at anything that you won't pull the trigger on!"

So the two dogs got them in position on the firing range. "Bentley you are to go first." ordered the Corporal. A huge smile came across Bentley as he turned to Dutch "watch this!" he told Dutch. It was at this point Bentley should've checked whether or not the machine gun was on fully auto or not? He aimed down the barrel at the target, concentrated then proceeded to squeeze the trigger and in a

CASE FILE:- The New Guard

matter of a few seconds the gun was empty. Bentley was dazed by the recoil of the gun partially, but also at the fact for all the bullets he had fired at the target not one had actually connected and hit the target!!

Dutch had burst in to laughter at Bentleys expense by this point, so a now embarrassed Bentley sharply said to Dutch "Your turn, let's see if you can do any better?" as he proceeded to walk away with the hump.

CASE FILE:- The New Guard

Corporal Mac Hamish

Elite Sniper

Serial number: 246899

Gender: Male

Breed: Scottish Deer hound

Age: 8 years

Dutch took up his rifle then looked down the sights, but due to him still giggling as he pulled the trigger the bullets missed the target. "Wait a second and calm yourself" came the Corporals voice from over Dutch's shoulder. "When you're ready just gently squeeze the trigger" the Corporal added. Dutch relaxed and took his time then squeezed the trigger, boom and there was the bullet hole off to

CASE FILE:- The New Guard

one side of the centre of the target. Dutch was delighted he actually hit the target! Even Bentley was delighted for him he came over and shook his paw. "Well we have some work to do, but you have potential." the Corporal told them. Bentley still a bit moody from his earlier experience asked the Corporal "Well how good are you then?" The Corporal turned to Dutch and asked "May I borrow your rifle please?" "Certainly Corporal" replied Dutch as he handed him the rifle.

"Ok lads, you've been shooting out to 100 metres, you see the back targets?" The two of them peered into the distance where they could just about make out some targets. "Yes" they replied. "That's 1000

CASE FILE:- The New Guard

metres." The Corporal informed. Bentley responded "That's not possible. I'll even wager that if you hit it you can have my lunch as well as your own." "Okay, I'll take your bet young private and if I miss you can have mine, fair?" replied the Corporal. Bentley nodded in reply then stood back licking his lips with anticipation of the extra large lunch he was going to have that day. The Corporal placed himself in to position and took his time, for a second the two privates had actually thought he had fallen asleep on his rifle, but what they didn't know was the Corporal was slowing down his breathing so to produce a more accurate shot. Boom went the rifle and the Corporal lay for a second and then got to his feet. "Okay lads?" he

CASE FILE:- The New Guard

questioned. Bentley replied "it's too far away, we can't tell if you hit it or not?" The Corporal had moved to where the equipment was laying and picked up something in anticipation of their question. "There you go look through this." he told them, as he passed them a telescope. Dutch was the first to look through then said nothing except he now had a grin on his face. Bentley had at this point become impatient and took the telescope from Dutch. "Don't snatch, Bentley!" as Dutch reprimanded him. "Sorry. But there's a lot at stake here." Bentley replied. As Bentley brought the telescope up to his eye all he could think of was all that lovely food he was going to have for lunch. Bentley's face turned from joy to horror as he saw the results in

CASE FILE:- The New Guard

front of him. His jaw swung open, then a nervous twitch appeared on his lip as he stood back and handed the telescope back to the Corporal. What had caused such a reaction? The Corporal had not only hit the target, but put a bullet straight through the bull's eye!

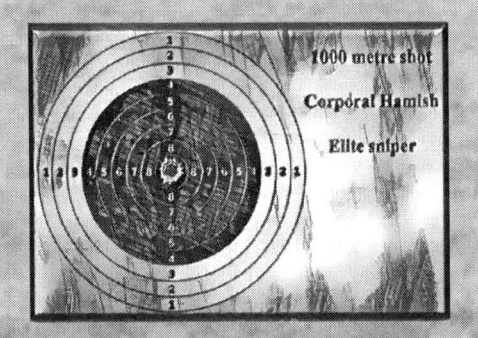

1000 metre shot
Corporal Hamish
Elite sniper

The Corporal glanced at Bentley and his reaction. "Well a deal is a deal. You won fair and square Corporal." Bentley announced then put out his paw to shake the Corporals paw to show good

CASE FILE:- The New Guard

sportsmanship. The Corporal shook his paw and quietly said to Bentley "never judge a book by its cover also never bet unless you know you will win. Have you learnt your lesson young Bentley?" "Yes Corporal." Bentley replied deflated. The Corporal looked him in the eye then said "don't worry you can have half of my lunch." he winked with a grin. Bentleys face lit up." thank you Corporal." he replied. The Corporal responded "well you've learnt your lesson, there's no need to punish you over it." as his grin turned to a smile. As the weeks went by our two heroes trained and trained until it was two weeks until they would know what unit they would go to. "I think we'll be in an infantry unit Bentley by the time we've finished this training."

CASE FILE:- The New Guard

Dutch told Bentley. "I'm hoping Canteen staff." Bentley replied. "You would!" Dutch answered rolling his eyes towards the heavens. As he rolled his eyes up he noticed the camp clock and realised the time. "Oh no!" "Come on we're going to be late, Corporal Nailer is waiting for us!" The two of them soon picked up their pace and ran to the other side of the camp to where Corporal Nailer was waiting. "Did we forget our meeting this morning?" "No of course not Corporal. We thought the exercise would do us some good on the way here." Dutch replied whilst trying to catch his breath. The Corporal waited until the pair of them had composed themselves and then announced that they would be doing gas mask training that morning. The two

CASE FILE:- The New Guard

privates looked at each other and wondered what was going to happen next?

The corporal handed them some gas masks and showed them how to put them on, then proceeded to order them in to a small hut. "Okay lads, once you're inside I'm going to throw this gas canister in, it will choke you and make your eyes water but don't worry it won't kill you. Give it 30 seconds and then put your masks on, I will tell you to come out. Okay?" "Yes Corporal" they both replied. The two privates went in to the hut, sat down and waited. The door opened, the Corporal pulled the pin on the gas canister then shouted "Gas, Gas, Gas!" then he proceeded to shut the door. Dutch and Bentley

CASE FILE:- The New Guard

carried on chatting as if nothing had happened.

The Corporal was watching the time on his watch and was awaiting for the two them to be falling out the door in distress, but nothing? He opened the door and stepped in, there was Dutch and Bentley mid conversation with no gas masks on? The poor Corporal was puzzled it must have been a dud canister, so he pulled the pin on another one with the same result? Okay, what is going on? He thought as he took of his gas mask, immediately due to two canisters being used the effects took hold, his eyes started to sting until he couldn't see and he was choking trying to get air. The two privates jumped in to action then dragged the poor

CASE FILE:- The New Guard

bedraggled Corporal out in to the fresh air and gave him a mug of water to help him wash his face and drink. "I don't understand?" The Corporal kept saying out loud. Dutch looked at Bentley and then looked at the poor Corporal and answered " I think I've built up an immunity due to shall we say Bentleys gas problems." Bentley looked sheepish then replied "I can't help it!" The Corporal shook his head in disbelief and ordered the pair of them off to lunch so he could carry on sorting himself out. So the two privates walked off towards the canteen still bickering about Bentley's diet and the effects of Bentley's bowel condition, Colitis. It was the day of passing out and today was the day they would now find out what unit they would be in.

CASE FILE:- The New Guard

As the passing out parade commenced the two privates hadn't noticed a figure that they had met earlier in their Army career so far, watching from the side lines.

The two privates passed out with flying colours at the parade, but were still wondering where they were going to go next? As they discussed the matter between themselves. "Afternoon gentlemen." a voice announced from behind them, in which they both recognised immediately. Both privates turned on their heels, came to attention and saluted the officer in front of them. "Afternoon Brigadier" they both replied. There in front of them stood Brigadier General Baggins. "So you two are

CASE FILE:- The New Guard

wondering what's next and why an old Brigadier like me had taken an interest in you?" "Well yes sir." Dutch answered. "Come with me. We have some travelling to do and once we reach our destination all will be revealed." The two of them fell in behind the Brigadier and followed him until they reached a car. As they approached the car a dog was waiting, in whom Dutch knew very well. Sergeant Rosa was at the rear of the car with the door open for Brigadier. "Thank you Rosa. Now let's get going we have some distance to cover." the Brigadier ordered then proceeded to sit in the car. "Come on you two, we haven't got all day!" he ordered Dutch and Bentley. "Yes sir, but what about our belongings?" Bentley asked. "Don't worry your

CASE FILE:- The New Guard

belongings will be follow. Now come on!" The
Brigadier replied a bit more sterner this time. Off
they went still not knowing what adventures
awaited them?

CASE FILE:- The New Guard

Chapter 5........ New beginnings.

They arrived at the base situated in London; they stepped out of the car feeling weary. The Brigadier ordered them to freshen up and also to have something to eat and drink. Once refreshed he would send Sergeant Rosa to fetch them to his office. Dutch and Bentley went off taking in the splendour of the old building they were walking through, when a Corporal intercepted them and took them to where they needed to be. Meanwhile Sergeant Rosa was discussing with the Brigadier about his decision to do with our two young privates. "Are you sure sir they are going to be up to the task?" Sergeant

CASE FILE:- The New Guard

Rosa asked. "I'm sure, Sergeant, I'm sure." he replied as they headed off to his office.

Some while later Sergeant Rosa found then escorted Bentley and Dutch to the Brigadiers office. The Sergeant knocked on his office door.

"Yes come in." the Brigadier ordered. They step in to a large grand office with a large desk at one end of the room with a huge leather chair. In the middle of the room was a large conference table with maps and files scattered around and to one side of the room was a large board with different information pinned to it. The three of them marched in, shut the door then marched to the large

CASE FILE:- The New Guard

desk at the end of the room where the Brigadier was sitting. They came to attention then saluted him; he acknowledged it then ordered them to stand easy. "Okay gentlemen you're wondering why I have brought you here and who I actually am?" the Brigadier asked. "Yes sir" replied Dutch. "Okay, pull up those chairs, it's time to listen." Sergeant Rosa moved to the other end of the room and started to look through some paperwork whilst the two privates pulled up their chairs, sat down and started to listen to the Brigadier.

The Brigadier proceeded to tell them that he had chosen them to join the Special Dog Squadron, a Special Forces unit that though small in number

CASE FILE:- The New Guard

had a powerful role within the Army and that within the squadron there are specialist divisions. He then went on to introduce himself properly, that his role within the regiment as the commanding officer. "So lads what do you think, are you up to the task? It will be dangerous mind you, but I think you have the hearts to get the job done." The Brigadier asked. Dutch looked at Bentley, Bentley nodded yes and Dutch answered "Yes sir, we're ready." "Good, good. Right there's some different rules here at the S.D.S. First you are both now Sergeants, so have the powers to go with the position. Secondly a tradition within the regiment is that Males grow a glorious moustache. There is a reason behind this and that is, there

CASE FILE:- The New Guard

will be times you won't be in uniform and the moustache commands respect where ever you go."

"Yes Sir." the now Sergeants replied. The Brigadier carried on explaining that the regiment is more relaxed than the regular Army so not to stand on parade all the time. After that he ordered them away to their rooms to relax and that they had a big day the next day.

Brigadier General Archibald Baggins

Commanding Officer - Special Dog Squadron - Watch Dog Division

Breed - Lakeland terrier

Serial number - 237512

Gender - Male

Age - 9 years

CASE FILE:- The New Guard

The two new Sergeants are walking the corridor towards their new rooms with Sergeant Rosa guiding them. "Bentley, can you believe that this happened?" Dutch asked Bentley. Bentley still trying to take it all in, replies "No, what have we done?" Rosa smiles then butts into their conversation, "Try not to worry, in all the years I have known the Brigadier I have never known him to make a mistake, but saying that there's always the first time?" she teased. Bentley looked Rosa in the eyes with a bemused look and just says "Thanks!" Dutch is the first to laugh and within a split second the three of them are laughing at Bentley's response.

CASE FILE:- The New Guard

The three of them reached the rooms. "Okay I'll see you two tomorrow, try to get some rest." Rosa said as she left the two of them for the night. "Goodnight." Dutch replied and "Goodnight to you to" Rosa replied before she exited out of sight. Dutch sighed as he watched Rosa leave." Hey you'll see her tomorrow." said Bentley. "I know." Dutch replied and with that they bid each other a goodnight then settled themselves down for the night.

They met at the Brigadiers office the next morning sporting their new Sergeant stripes on their uniform. Dutch started the conversation "Morning Sergeant." "Morning Sergeant." Bentley replied as

CASE FILE:- The New Guard

they both chuckled. "Okay that's enough you two." the Brigadier ordered. "Yes sir." Bentley replied. "Right, first of all you two you are still training and will be for some time as I mentioned to you yesterday the S.D.S is a special forces unit, it is among the elite, so there is no place for shoddy work here. Over the next Couple of months you will go off and train with different specialist Regiments to acquire the skills as full operational Operatives." "Yes sir" Dutch replied. "Good, Good. Well your first port of call is Portsmouth with the Marines, Captain Frank Billingham knows all about it, jolly good chap he is. Pick up your rail pass from Sergeant Rosa and I'll keep an eye on your progress. Go on get going." The Brigadier ordered.

CASE FILE:- The New Guard

The two sergeants done as the Brigadier ordered and off they went on a train from London to Portsmouth.

Dutch was quietly looking out the window of the train contemplating the journey they had begun and the reason why it had all started. His thoughts turned to his Master, his friend Kevin, his little heart sunk in worry at the thought of not knowing if Kevin was okay or even if he is still alive? No, he mustn't think like that. At that moment his chain of thoughts had been broken as the sight of Bentley entering the carriage gingerly carrying by the looks of it a six course meal with all the silver ware. Dutch just stared as Bentley artfully

CASE FILE:- The New Guard

juggled entire platters from a paw to paw whilst balancing a plate on his head. "What? I remembered your packet of crisps!" Bentley answered Dutch's look. Dutch just shook his head and laughed, "Do you need a paw?" "I'm fine thanks" Bentley replied as he was just about to stop an escaping sausage from rolling off the plate. "Got it!" Bentley said in triumph whilst now standing there with a sausage hanging out of his mouth that looked too similar to a cigar for Dutch's liking. "I wouldn't smoke that if I was you!" Dutch teased. Bentley was trying his hardest not to spit the sausage across the carriage in a fit of laughter. But with a bit of suction and a gulp he swallowed the sausage in one go!

CASE FILE:- The New Guard

The rest of the journey wasn't as eventful, but it did give the pair of them some time to relax and after many hours the train arrived at Portsmouth station. They both left the train then proceeded to make their way to the entrance of the station, there waiting for them was Captain Billingham. "Welcome to Portsmouth gentlemen, I will be looking after you during your stay with us, any questions?" the Captain asked them. "No sir, we're fine." Dutch replied. "Okay, well follow me, we'll soon have you back to the base." the Captain ordered and off they went following the Captain all the way to the base that was situated by the sea. "Wow!" the two sergeants let out in an amazement. "What is it?" The Captain enquired. "Sorry sir, but

CASE FILE:- The New Guard

we've never seen the sea before, only in pictures. It smells so good!" Dutch replied. The Captain realising it was their first time by the sea responded "We have some time, let's go down to the beach and you can see what it's like." The three of them went out on to the beach. "I see it every day and I had forgotten what a wonderful place it actually is. You have 10 minutes Sergeants to explore and relax." "Thank you sir." the two Sergeants replied, so off they went running up and down the beach whilst the Captain just sat down for a moment to take in the beauty that was around him.

CASE FILE:- The New Guard

Bentley was chasing Dutch, whilst Dutch was ducking and weaving just out of reach of him. Then Dutch aimed towards the sea at full pelt and ran as hard as could, Bentley was hot on his heels, then suddenly Dutch's paws hit the water he sprung straight up in the air leaving enough room for Bentley to pass completely under him.

Captain Frank Billingham

Marine - Special Operations

Breed: Otter hound

Serial number: 242151

Gender: Male

Age: 8 years

Special Mention: Awarded Dickin Medal for Bravery.

CASE FILE:- The New Guard

Bentley due to his size and mass couldn't stop as quick so went crashing face first in to the waves. A few moments later Bentley came to the surface coughing and spluttering, "Something has got me!" in a panic stricken voice as he raced to the beach, then proceeded to run up and down the beach paws flailing try to disentangle whatever that was holding him. Dutch looked panicked so was racing beside his friend trying to help him. The Captain just sat there laughing at the sight of the two sergeants running up and down the beach, but in the end he got up and calmed them down. "Wait! Stop!" the Captain ordered as Bentley and Dutch were fighting with the unknown attacker. They both stopped what they were doing. "Right, what we have

CASE FILE:- The New Guard

here is Kelp sea weed." the Captain informed as he laughed. "Sea weed?" Bentley asked. "Yes sea weed, it grows in the sea just like grass grows on land." the Captain replied still laughing. "Hmm, you mean I was scared of grass!" Bentley replied as he finally pulled it off and dropped it on the beach then stared at it with disgust." "Come on, let's get going" ordered the Captain. "Be right with you Sir" Dutch replied, Dutch turned to Bentley and said "Come on, just leave it alone." Bentley replied "Grass, it was grass!" "I'll give it being grass!" Dutch warns him "Bentley. No just leave it!" Bentley ignores him and proceeds to urinate on it and then kicks it up the beach! "Did you have to?"

CASE FILE:- The New Guard

Dutch asks "Yep. Now its sea weed" replies Bentley as he walked of triumphantly up the beach.

The Marines base was similar to the other base they had been on but there was a definitely a Naval feeling to it as well, which really wasn't strange as the marines are at home in the water as they are on land. Over the weeks at the camp the two sergeants learnt swimming techniques, how to use canoes, boats and many other commando techniques in which would all come in useful in their military careers ahead of them.

It was the last day at the camp and our two heroes had got up early so headed for the beach for the last time to watch the sunrise over the sea. As

CASE FILE:- The New Guard

they sat on the beach as dawn broke they recognised a figure strolling towards them, it was Captain Billingham. "Morning lads, I thought you might be here." as introduced his arrival. "Yes sir, we thought we would just take it all in one last time," replied Dutch. "I don't blame you, but remember you have your test later and once done please report to my office." "Yes sir the two Sergeants replied and Captain Billingham carried on his stroll back to the camp.

The test was hard going as it was a combination of all the skills they had learnt whilst being at the camp, but they succeed. Once they were finished they carried out their order and promptly reported

CASE FILE:- The New Guard

to Captain Billingham's office. They knocked on his door and he beckoned them in to his office. The office was of a reasonable size with a desk and chairs, but something had caught both the Sergeants eyes, it was a framed medal hanging on the wall. The Captain noticed their interest in the frame. "Would you like to look at it?" the Captain asked. "Yes sir, please if that's okay?" replied Bentley. The Captain took the frame down and passed it to them across the desk to them. The two sergeants took hold of it and examined it. "Wow sir this is a Dickins medal!" said Bentley. "Yes it is Sergeant Bentley." "May I ask how did you receive the medal Sir?" Dutch enquired. "Let's just say I done my duty on the day and a few humans are still alive because

CASE FILE:- The New Guard

of it, Ok?" "Yes sir" Dutch replied, as he gazed down knowing the immense bravery that Captain Billingham must of shown to be awarded such a medal he was wondering to himself whether or not he could ever be so brave and courageous like Captain Billingham?

"Enough about me and the past." said the Captain as he took back the frame and hung it back on the wall. "Today is about your achievements. I have

CASE FILE:- The New Guard

been in contact with Brigadier Baggins and discussed everything about your training and your results." the Captain informed them. The two Sergeants just stood and listened to what the captain was saying. Bentley was hoping the incident about the methane explosion in the camp latrines would not be mentioned. The captain carried on informing them "After careful thought and consideration due to passing your commando training and showing tremendous leadership skills Sergeant Dutch you have been promoted to the rank of Major. Sergeant Bentley" Bentleys heart sunk after thinking about the methane explosion. "Sergeant Bentley due to passing your commando training and also after investigations in to the methane

CASE FILE:- The New Guard

explosion episode and how you saved the camp by your actions you awarded a promotion to Captain and awarded the brown star medal for services beyond the norm." The two new promoted officers stood there trying to take it in. Dutch shook the Captains paw and Bentley followed suit, they then turned and congratulated one another over their achievements. The Captain spoke up "before you go, I have something for you both to remember us by and as you earned it." He then proceeded to open his draw then produced two commando daggers plus two patches and handed them to the two new officers. "Thank you captain" they both replied. "As I said you earned them, wear the patches with pride." the Captain answered them.

CASE FILE:- The New Guard

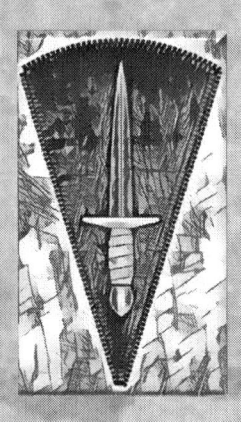

The next day the two new offices left the base and travelled back to London to find out where their training would take them next?

"Okay gentlemen if you could wait in the library, I will inform the Brigadier that you have arrived" the Sergeant informed Dutch and Bentley. They both stepped into the library and were amazed at the size of the room which had a real old gentlemen's club feel to it, with leather chairs and volumes

CASE FILE:- The New Guard

upon volumes of books everywhere. As they scanned the room they noticed a fireplace and beside it was a large leather chair with an elderly dog a sleep in it. They moved towards the fire place and all of a sudden the old dog awoke with a start "Large Badger, Fingerless gloves!" he shouted Dutch and Bentley stared in disbelief? The next they knew they were diving for cover as the old dog had reached down the side of his chair and proceeded to fire a blunderbuss in their direction! As the smoke from the discharged gun started to clear they quickly saw a huge hole in a once pristine shelve of books! Before they could even say anything a Sergeant ran in to the room and gently wrestled the gun out of the old dog's paws and swapped it for

CASE FILE:- The New Guard

a glass of port. "There you go sir, let me take your gun and reload it for you. Here's a glass of port whilst you wait" the sergeant said as he winked to the two officers. Dutch and Bentley were still in shock and couldn't believe what was going on? The next they knew Brigadier Baggins entered the room. "Morning gentlemen, I see you've met Colonel Butteriss." the brigadier announced. "Ah, yes sir you could say that!" replied Dutch. "Oh don't mind him, he's the last of the old guard, he's seen a lot in his career and has never been the same after his stint in Africa."

CASE FILE:- The New Guard

Colonel Maynard Butterriss

Special Dog Squadron

Breed: Blue Paul Terrier (last of)

Serial number: 23000

Gender: Male

Age: 14 years?

Special Mention: Knight of the Order of the brown star

The brigadier informed them. By this point Colonel Butterriss had swallowed his port and fallen back to sleep again. The Brigadier carried on "See he's harmless." Dutch and Bentley just stared at the hole in the library wall in disbelief and replied "Yes Sir?" The Brigadier carried on the conversation by informing them that they would be

CASE FILE:- The New Guard

off to finish their final part of their training North of London to an Aerodrome at Old Warden in Bedfordshire in which they will be under the tutorage of Wing Commander Robbie Burns.

Dutch and Bentley were looking forward to arriving at Old Warden as it wasn't far from their home and it would be their first time back in some while.

They arrived at the local train station to Aerodrome where they were collected then brought in front of the Wing commander. The wing commander introduces himself "Afternoon gentlemen, I'm wing commander Burns and I will be your instructor for the next few weeks in which I will teach you how to fly and you will earn your wings

CASE FILE:- The New Guard

as a S.D.S Operative." The two young officers look around them at the different aeroplanes in awe.

As they stood the in the hanger their awe soon turned to concern as they inspected these aeroplanes and then realised that all that was going to keep them from plummeting to ground was wood and cloth! Bentley asked the Wing Commander "Sir are they safe to fly?" The Wing Commander smirked "Yes as safe as houses and of course you have plenty of time to think about that question when you plummet from 10,000 feet!" Bentleys jaw just swung open and started to blabber "10,000ft!" Dutch didn't help the situation by teasing Bentley by mentioning the outcome would be like a large

CASE FILE:- The New Guard

dollop of strawberry jam and that it would take one large butter knife to clean up the mess. Once the teasing had died down Wing Commander advised them to settle in to their barracks and to meet him the next day for the start of their lessons.

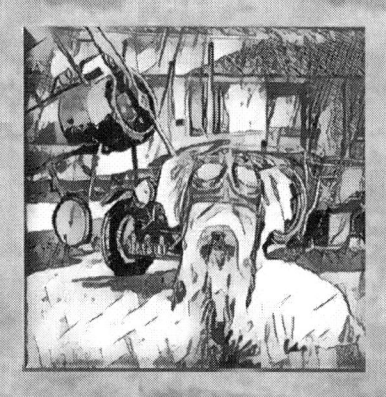

Wing Commander Robbie Burns
Canine Air Force Pilot
Breed: Skye terrier
Serial number: 23797
Gender: Male
Age: 9 years

The next morning the Captain and Major were waiting in the class room, Bentley is discussing with Dutch why these new flying contraptions are

CASE FILE:- The New Guard

the Devils work. The Door opens and the Wing Commander makes his way in to the classroom, "morning gentlemen I hope you're both well rested as it's going to be a busy day?" he asked. "Yes Wing commander, we're fine." replied Dutch. Bentley looked at him in astonishment; thinking to himself has nothing I've just said sunk in? "Right then let's get on with Basics shall we." Burns instructed them. "First of all this is a bird," as he pointed to a number of pictures on the class room wall." This is an Aeroplane, it goes up and down in the air like a bird, but for your sake you don't flap your paws." "Following so far?" he asked, Dutch and Bentley looked at each other and turned nodded yes and he carried on. "This is us" as he pointed to a

CASE FILE:- The New Guard

picture of a green plane" and this is the enemy."
"Both got that?" "You don't shoot at the green
ones!" Our heroes just nodded in agreement.

Canine Air force Identity Picture

1. Bird Flying (Not an Aeroplane!)

Canine Air force Identity Picture

1. British Aeroplane (GREEN!)

CASE FILE:- The New Guard

> Canine Air force Identity Picture
>
> 1. German Aeroplane (RED!)
>
> SHOOT!

"Right that's your lesson done, let's go flying!" Burns informed them. "What?" Bentley shrieked "That's it, that's the lesson?" he carried on. The Wing Commander looked stunned and replied defensively "I've given you the extended lesson don't you know, most pilots don't even get shown the difference between a pigeon and aeroplane!" "Oh great, that makes all the difference, I feel so much safer with that knowledge!" Replied Bentley

CASE FILE:- The New Guard

sarcastically. "Great glad we got that little misunderstanding out the way, let's get going it looks like we have good weather." the Wing Commander replied as he proceeded to venture out of the classroom and on to the grass airstrip. As Dutch and Bentley followed the Wing Commander out all you could hear from Bentley was "I feel so much more reassured that we had the extended lesson!" as he kept shaking his head in disbelief.

"Ok who's coming up with me first?" the Wing Commander asked. Before Dutch had a chance to answer Bentley had taken two steps back so leaving left Dutch front and centre. "That's the spirit!" said the Wing Commander, Dutch looked puzzled until

CASE FILE:- The New Guard

he realised what Bentley had done. "Yes sir, be right with you, I'm just putting on my flying helmet." replied Dutch. The Wing Commander also asked "You have used the extra strong moustache wax haven't you? There's nothing worse than being moustached slapped mid flight you know." Dutch reached for his tin of Moustache wax and applied a liberal amount to his moustache, just to be on the safe side. "All done Wing Commander," Dutch answered. "Good, Good, let's get up there" The Wing Commander ordered.

So off they went in a dual control Biplane. The Wing Commander took off then proceeded to attain some altitude before handing the controls over to

CASE FILE:- The New Guard

Dutch. Dutch was nervous and listened intensely to all the instruction given.

Bentley had found a sunny spot to sit and watch the training in progress and was looking around the airfield when he noticed something unusual so he went off to investigate. On the side of the air field was a large impression of what looked like an aeroplane burnt in to the grass. A passing mechanic noticed Bentleys curiosity and yelled over to him "Yes that was a good one, faulty fuel line, didn't half go up, we were still cooking our jacket potatoes in the embers that evening." as he carried on walking to a hanger. Bentley just stood there dumbfounded thinking to himself I know I like

CASE FILE:- The New Guard

jacket potatoes but I certainly don't want to be one! He returned to where he was originally sitting pondering on what had happened and had the image of the jacket potatoes cooking away in his mind. It's no good I have to go and have something to eat all this talking of food has made me hungry as he got up and made his way to the canteen.

Dutch at this stage had started to relax and was enjoying his lesson he was looking forward to landing and telling his friend all about it. As they landed Bentley wasn't in sight, Dutch reassured the Wing Commander that Bentley was probably in the latrines and he would go and look for him. As Dutch started to head for the latrines

CASE FILE:- The New Guard

around the corner came Bentley with a huge sausage roll in his paw and was busily trying to eat it. "Where did you get that from?" asked Dutch. "Oh a guy called Greg in the canteen, he asked if I would like to try one of his sausage rolls, I couldn't say no, it would've been rude to do so." Bentley replied as he carried on tucking in to the now almost finished sausage roll. Dutch rolled his eyes to the heavens and answered "trust you, you just cannot say no to a sausage roll can you?" "No." Bentley replied looking embarrassed. "Come on it's your turn to go up." Dutch reminded him. "Okay, okay!" Bentley replied as dragged his heels all the way to the aeroplane.

CASE FILE:- The New Guard

Bentley was popping the last of the sausage roll in to his mouth as he sat down in the Biplane. Up until this point in time the comfort of eating had taken his mind off of his earlier fears, that was until they left the runway and started to climb to altitude. Bentley had his eyes closed all the way up then once reaching a safe height the Wing Commander instructed that he was handing the controls over to Bentley. It was at this point that Bentley had regretted not putting a clean handkerchief in his pocket as Dutch always advises him, as due to just eating a very greasy sausage roll he was now having trouble gripping the controls. The Biplane went back and forth up and down as he struggled to retain any form of control

CASE FILE:- The New Guard

of the biplanes steering. Just as he thought he now had some control the worst thing could of happened, he had forgotten to apply extra strong wax to his moustache and was now being viscously slapped by his own moustache. Bentley ducked and weaved trying to miss the blows and so doing so the plane would roll about in the air till at one point the biplane was upside down, which did give Bentley a reprieve from being slapped as gravity was holding his moustache down. "Okay I have the Controls" instructed the Wing Commander as he righted the biplane and bought it back to land. As soon as the biplane landed Bentley jumped out and started kissing the ground. "Oh it so nice to be back on the ground" Bentley kept repeating. "Good show Bentley,

CASE FILE:- The New Guard

you mastered the plane like an old pro, well done" the wing commander informed him. Bentley glanced up in amazement then replied "thank you" and then proceeded to collapse. "Right I'll see you two tomorrow for the same again." the Wing commander informed them and of he went to the barracks.

It didn't take too long before both the Captain and Major were starting to fly solo without further incidents happening to poor old Bentley.

So we return to the beginning where the Captain and Major are discussing their training so that they can go to the front to hopefully to meet up with Kevin their master and friend.

CASE FILE:- The New Guard

"Yes the quicker we can complete this training the quicker the Brigadier will send us on our first mission to the front I'm sure." Dutch informed Bentley. Bentley agreed and so they set out to complete their training as soon as possible, as all they knew that something terrible had happened, they desperately wanted to help if they could.

The last few weeks flew by and accomplished their training with fly colours. As they were about to leave and say farewell to the Wing Commander he had a message and a surprise for them. "First of all gentlemen may I congratulate you both for achieving your wings in record time, jolly good show." the wing commander told them, then carried

CASE FILE:- The New Guard

on " The Brigadier has been informed of your achievement and he's sent up a little surprise for you both, follow me." They walked from his office around to a nearby hanger and he open the door to reveal a small three wheeled car! "This is from the Brigadier to you both as an operation vehicle. You must of seriously impressed him to receive such a gift." The wing commander informed them. "Wow. We must of!" replied Bentley. "What is it?" "Asked Dutch. The Wing Commander produced some paperwork and proceeded to read, "Ah it's a Morgan racing car, developed this year and had to be put on hold due to the war, so they have donated it to the S.D.S as a an operational vehicle, it certainly looks quick and it does 200 miles before you need

CASE FILE:- The New Guard

The 1914 Morgan Racing Car donated by Morgan to The Special Dog Squadron.

to fill the petrol tank again!" He informed them. Bentleys eyes had glazed over he was in love with this new car, "Can I drive it? Please, can I drive it?" Bentley asked. Dutch looked at him, he was like a new puppy with a bone, how could he say no. "Of course old friend" Dutch replied with a warm smile. "Thank you," replied Bentley as he jumped in to the driver's seat and started the engine

CASE FILE:- The New Guard

ready to go. Dutch turned to the wing commander and thanked him for all his kindness plus tuition. He then climbed in to the seat beside Bentley and they started to pull away, as they drove off Bentley noticed the car had a horn and squeezed it POOP, POOP it made Dutch jump! "Well that will move people out the way!" said Bentley whilst laughing his head off.

They drove out of old warden, Dutch had a map on his lap and directed Bentley to the old London road once on the road they made great haste towards London with Bentley POOP, POOPING other road users to move as they approached, so were back in London in record time.

CASE FILE:- The New Guard

The Morgan SDS operations vehicle with
Captain Poopstacker 1914

CASE FILE:- The New Guard

Chapter six..... Secrets revealed

The Brigadier was waiting in his office for our heroes to arrive; he couldn't miss them as he had heard Bentley POOP, POOPING the sentry at the gate as he drove through in to the Barracks.

"Ah good day gentlemen." the Brigadier announced as Bentley and Dutch entered his office. "Good day sir." they replied as they moved towards the chairs in front of the Brigadiers desk. "Yes pull up chair and sit down lads." the Brigadier told them. Both Dutch and Bentley thanked him then proceeded to sit down and relax after their long drive. The Brigadier asked "How's the new car from Morgan?"

CASE FILE:- The New Guard

"Great, it's really fast!" replied Bentley with excitement. "Good, good. It was very kind of Morgan to donate the car, so look after it." the Brigadier told them and then carried on "Also the horn, did you read the paperwork that I sent you?" The two officers looked sheepish, "No sir, we haven't had an opportunity yet sir." Dutch replied. The Brigadier looked at Bentley and proceeded to instruct him on the use of the horn, that it had been developed to sound different than normal so that other road users and police officers would know it was an emergency so to move out of their way, not to be used to see how high they could make people jump! Bentley took on board what the Brigadier had told

CASE FILE:- The New Guard

him and promised to keep his POOP POOPING to a minimum.

"Okay gentlemen your training has brought you to this point in time and it is time that we have to discuss." the Brigadier informed them. The two friends stood there puzzled, but carried on listening. "Right, I shall now inform you of top secret information in which only the chosen few know of the truth! At the beginning of our time with man our ancestors had an incident with a human time traveller from far, far in to the future that had come back in time and then proceeded to bestow on our ancestors a heavy burden. This time traveller was concerned about the

CASE FILE:- The New Guard

path mankind may take without our help and guidance. Our ancestors agreed with him and so he imparted his wisdom to help us on our mission. Due to their position and guidance the Humans called our ancestors Watch Dogs, forever keeping an eye on the human's welfare. As that wasn't enough, the time traveller also gave us the means to change the time lines if we feel the Humans had gone too far due to sometimes their short sightedness and so creating a chain of events that would be catastrophic for them and as well as the whole world! As a result he left us these, the time collars and the library of time. The time collars give us the ability to travel back in time and change events if the time lines have been disrupted

CASE FILE:- The New Guard

too much. So that we know what the true chain of events are or supposed to be we have the Library which is shielded from time it's self. This could be the main reason why Colonel Butteriss basically lives in there. We still have no idea how old he actually is? But for all his eccentricities he's hub of information. So there you are Gentlemen, a lot to digest I know!" The Brigadier calmly explained. Dutch and Bentley just stood there in shock, then Dutch replied "Really, Okay is this April fool's day and no one has told us?" "It's all true" the Brigadier replied as he lent over the desk laying a dog collar in front of them on to his desk. There in front of them sat a collar with a device attached to it which looked like a pocket watch and

CASE FILE:- The New Guard

there were buttons on the sides of collar with Watch dog emblems on them. "So we can travel in to the future then?" said an excited Bentley. "NO! It is strictly forbidden for any Operative to travel to the future the knowledge they could come back with is to dangerous." snapped the Brigadier. "So this brings me to our largest peril yet in our history, someone has stolen one of our Time collars!" he carried on nervously.

Watch Dog Division Time Collar
Authorised personal only!

TOP SECRET AT THE HIGHEST LEVEL

Time collar only to be issued to authorised Watch Dog Operatives!

Specification:

Time travel

Communication device

CASE FILE:- The New Guard

The magnitude and seriousness of the matter hadn't sunk in with Bentley who was still envisioning what it must be like in the future? Dutch asked the question how was it stolen? They found out a Watch Dog Operator had been killed in France on a mission when the collar had been stolen. The Brigadier stood thinking about the operative and the situation for a few moments. "Okay you two, come with me" he ordered, then proceeded to march out of his office and straight to the library.

Colonel Butterriss was awake this time as they entered the library. "Afternoon Colonel," as the Brigadier introduced himself, "Yes sir, afternoon." he replied "Anything to report so far?" The

CASE FILE:- The New Guard

Brigadier asked. "Not so far sir." Butterriss replied. Colonel Butterriss was sat at a large desk inspecting a huge book in front of him. Dutch was the first to ask the question "Sir, what is he doing?" "Glad you asked." the Brigadier replied "He's inspecting the time lines to see if anyone has changed events in the past that we haven't noticed yet." the colonel carried on. Dutch and Bentley stood next to the desk to be able to get a better look of what the colonel was looking at. "It's like looking at a road map sir!" Bentley said in surprise. "Yes very similar." The old Colonel replied "But the lines are moving on the page!"Bentley carried on. The Colonel replied

CASE FILE:- The New Guard

again "Yes as time waits for no one..Well may be me.." he replied with an old wiry smile. The Brigadier explained to the two young officers that every line is a matter of importance to the human race development and that one decision or instant could change the direction of that line. "So as you can see this last year the lines have been wriggling and turning a lot due to the great war as decisions are made. The Colonel is keeping his eyes open for any major change in direction from the norm."

After a lengthy spell with the Colonel, the Brigadier was happy that the Time collar hadn't been used yet! "Right you two, I have disclosed the

CASE FILE:- The New Guard

secret of the Watch Dog Division to you a lot sooner than I had anticipated, but due to the circumstances you are now part of the division and full operatives, any questions?" The brigadier asked Dutch and Bentley. Dutch replied as Bentley was annoying the Colonel by sitting in his favourite chair and drinking his Port. "I think we're ready sir." as he glanced around then saw what Bentley was up to and then Dutch fell silent. "What do you think Colonel?" asked the Brigadier, "Yes, yes just get him out of here," as the Colonel pointed at Bentley as Bentley had found the Colonels Blunder buss!

CASE FILE:- The New Guard

They left the library all too quickly and if it wasn't for the time pocket of the library that separated it from time, they were sure they would still be hearing the Colonel cussing about Bentley.

Back in the Brigadiers office he went through the instruction of the time collar, the object that looked like a pocket watch was the time navigation control, one side was for Year, month, day and the other side was hours, minutes, seconds. You pulled the winder up until it clicked once, then moved the hands for setting of the time coordinates for one side and you pulled it up another notch for the other side to adjust the hands to complete coordinates, once done you pushed the winder back

CASE FILE:- The New Guard

down and you will instantly be taken to that time coordinates. "I'm not sure?" asked Bentley. "Okay, we'll do a short trip" replied the Brigadier. He set the time collar to three hours in the past, and then handed it to Bentley. "Push the winder down" as the Brigadier had said it Bentley had disappeared. Dutch panicked and was concerned for his friend. The Brigadier reassured him that he was fine and he will be back in an instant. Bentley appeared again and was laughing his head off. "What's so funny?" Dutch asked "I've just watched me Poop Pooping the sentry again from this morning," replied Bentley chuckling to himself. "Bentley!" the Brigadier was about to warn him. "I know sir, I

CASE FILE:- The New Guard

know, you've told me more than three times now sir." Bentley replied.

The brigadier carried on to explain that the communication device can be used through time and that the receiver is in the library to be in a stable position in case any thing was to go wrong with time.

After some further instruction the Brigadier issued them both with time collars and new ID wallets almost identical to his own. The ID wallets were miniature time pockets that anchored you to the original time line so you would have recollection of the original time line.

CASE FILE:- The New Guard

There was a knock at the door and Sergeant Rosa entered carrying some files, "Sir, we have some new intelligence from C.I.9." Rosa informed. She handed the files to the Brigadier, "Great let me have look." the Brigadier replied as he opened the case file. "C.I.9 sir?" asked Dutch. "Yes, yes they're the spy chaps who keep us and the government informed, Canine Intelligence Nine to be exact." The Brigadier explained.

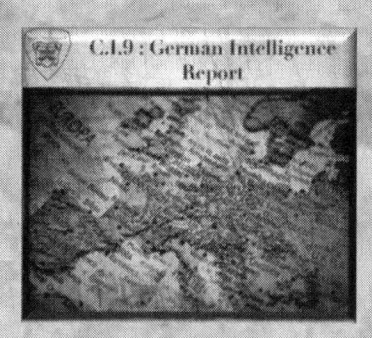

C.I.9 : German Intelligence Report

CLASSIFIED INTELLIGENCE REPORT.

Last known location of Watch Dog Operative from recovered German documents.

CASE FILE:- The New Guard

By deciphering the report from captured German spies we now know the time collar was last seen on the outskirts of Paris being moved towards the front lines of the Allied forces in France.

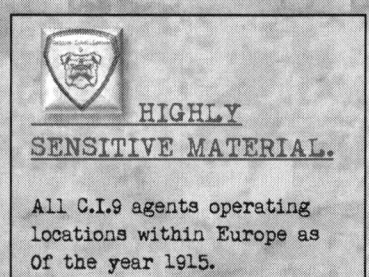

C.I.9 : Agent Location Report

HIGHLY SENSITIVE MATERIAL.
All C.I.9 agents operating locations within Europe as Of the year 1915.

From the combined information the Brigadier ordered for the two of them to head off to Amsterdam in the Netherlands to meet up with a C.I.9 agent Dani De Marie and her man servant Grunt for more information and to track down then return the time collar to him before it is used.

CASE FILE:- The New Guard

Dutch and Bentley hurriedly packed for their adventure and whilst doing so Dutch wondered if this was finally their chance of seeing Kevin?

Their belongings packed in to the Morgan and a quick check to make sure Bentley had plenty of clean underwear and clean hankies, they were ready. The Brigadier wished them Gods speed and off they roared to Harwich to meet up with a Royal Navy ship to take them across the sea.

CASE FILE:- The New Guard

Chapter 7.......... Time waits for no one.

The Morgan had sped across to Harwich and after a short wait the car had been craned on to the ship. Bentley went around inspecting the car just in case the Navy had damaged it in any way? "Will you calm yourself, it's perfectly Okay" Dutch told him. "But I'm sure they've scratched her!" replied Bentley, "Her?" Dutch asked. "Yes she's beautiful to me." replied Bentley, "Never mind" Dutch replied bemused at the situation.

The sea crossing had been choppy and so Bentley had spent most of the time with the Morgan making sure it wasn't being damaged at all by the rolling waves

CASE FILE:- The New Guard

and at times Dutch was sure he had heard Bentley talking to the car reassuring it!?

Once they arrived at the Port in Amsterdam they quickly disembarked, then once when finally they were reunited with the Morgan they set off to find and meet with the C.I.9 agent Dani De Marie. After a few stops for directions they finally pulled up outside a Cafe and checked the address, yes this was the place.

CASE FILE:- The New Guard

C.I.9 Head Agent

Name- Dani De Marie

Cover-Entertainer

Location- Amsterdam Netherlands

Abilities- Espionage, Spying and Misinformation.

C.I.9 Agent

Name- Grunt

Cover- None.

Location- Amsterdam Netherlands.

Abilities- Servant to Dani De Marie.

Inside amongst the customers sat a Poodle and a small Pug in conversation, as Dutch and Bentley

CASE FILE:- The New Guard

stepped towards them Dutch over heard the Pug say "they're here Mistress!" The pug got up and stood in between Dutch and the Poodle. In a calm tone the Poodle spoke "It's fine Grunt, let the Gentlemen sit down and refresh after their journey, would you like a drink?" Dutch and Bentley sat down whilst Grunt went off with their drink orders. "Please excuse Grunt, what he lacks in brains he makes up in courage. So let me introduce myself I'm Dani De Marie, but you can call me Dani" as the Poodle introduced herself, then carried on " So the SDS needs my help, what would you like to know?"

CASE FILE:- The New Guard

Dutch and Dani discussed the situation and Dani revealed new information that a German spy Fredrick Die Wurst was making his way back towards German controlled territory near to a French town called Saissons, North East of Paris. The only other piece of information they had was a photo of the spy to go by.

C.I.9 Intelligence Report

Intelligence category- German Spy

Name - Fredrick Die Wurst

Active Location - Paris France

Skill set - Master of disguise

CASE FILE:- The New Guard

Meanwhile on the outskirts of Paris Fredrick Die Wurst had been waiting in a safe house for the right moment to move towards the Allied front lines. Fredrick studied the map he had of the Saissons area and was deciding the best way to cross. Hmm he thought I can't walk across as the French will see me and I'll be captured, if I fly I could be shot down!

Hmm, I'm going to have to tunnel under the line, it will take me longer but it will be safer. Okay I will need a British uniform and papers for the mission. So Fredrick went off to acquire all the equipment he may need.

CASE FILE:- The New Guard

Back in Amsterdam Dutch and Bentley had decided to use the Royal Navy to transport them to Dunkirk and then follow the Allied line to the town of Saissons.

They said their goodbyes to Dani De Marie and set off on the Navy ship to Dunkirk.

Once at Calais they headed to the nearest English Head Quarters for the latest update on the Allied lines to make sure they didn't drive in to enemy held territory without them knowing it. They gathered the intelligence then worked out that either side really hadn't moved more than 6ft either way for the last month! Dutch turned to Bentley and told him of his plan that if they drove

CASE FILE:- The New Guard

down to a town called Arras and stay the night they should reach Saissons by the next day, Bentley agreed. With Bentley checking the Morgan over and refuelling it they were ready to go. "All set?" Dutch asked "Yes she's already to go, but I don't think much of these roads though!" Bentley replied as he pointed to the tight narrow lanes designed for a horse and cart. "Well I trust yours and the Morgan's abilities Bentley" Dutch replied with a confident nod.

The journey was hard and nerve wrecking as they made their way to Arras. "Boom, Boom, Boom" as the Allied Artillery was firing on to the German lines and then the German Artillery would fire back the

CASE FILE:- The New Guard

explosions were not very close but the vibrations from the explosions were making the little car skip backwards and forwards across the road, that and any horses encountered on their travels were terrified by the explosions, so Bentley had to keep his wits about him to make sure they stayed on the road without an accident occurring.

Bentley was pushing the Morgan to the limits, the little car was flying along, he was making sure that they reached their destination before night fall, not that Bentley was worried about driving in the dark, no his stomach was growling and the thought of another few hours without something to eat was spurring him on as he approached a large

CASE FILE:- The New Guard

hill. As he reached the top of the hill they could see some figures standing in the road with guns. Bentley brought the car to a standstill; Dutch observed the figures and couldn't make out who they were. They could be French, British or the Germans? Dutch ordered Bentley to take it slowly as they approached and to act natural, but if there was any trouble they would have to get out of there fast as their mission was too important to be held up. Bentley slowly moved the car towards the figures trying to identify who they were? Dutch suddenly recognised the spike on top of one the soldiers helmets, "Germans!" he told Bentley. Bentley looked about to see if he could turn around? After a quick look, nowhere in sight that

CASE FILE:- The New Guard

was suitable. Bentley looked at Dutch and just said "Don't worry I've got this!"

The German soldiers were positioned at the bottom of the road at a cross roads. Bentley revved up the Morgan's little engine pulled down his flying goggles, he was ready, Dutch followed suit and Bentley released the brakes. Off they went the engine screaming as they built up more and more speed, as they approached the first two soldiers on the road Bentley aimed the car to go in between them. The guards saw them coming and started to shout for the car to stop, they began to raise their guns as a warning, but it was too late the car was almost on top of them, there was a POOP, POOP and

CASE FILE:- The New Guard

they had to dive in to the hedge to escape being run over! Bentley didn't help their embarrassment by poop, pooping as he went past and then saluting them for good measure.

Bentley was over the moon that they had got through safely, "See I told you all the POOP, POOPING practice would come in handy one day!" He informed Dutch; Dutch was laughing and replied "Yes, yes well done my old friend, I'm proud of you."

An hour later the Morgan pulled in to the town and the two of them were looking for some where to stay the night, when they came across a little inn that looked perfect. They both ate and were ready

CASE FILE:- The New Guard

to go to bed after a long day, when Bentley
disappeared outside, Dutch wondered what Bentley
was up to and followed him to make sure he didn't
get himself in to trouble. But his fears came to
nothing as Bentley had driven the Morgan to a
stable and put the car under cover for the night.
Dutch was expecting for Bentley to return to the
Inn for the night, but Bentley had made up a straw
bed beside the Morgan for himself. Dutch looked
around the stable door; there was Bentley fast
asleep next to the Morgan! Dutch thought to
himself, I'm sure Bentley is in love with that car!
Oh well best not disturb him. So Dutch left Bentley
to his nights rest in the stables and made his own

CASE FILE:- The New Guard

way to his bed to which it wasn't long before he fell in to a heavy sleep.

CASE FILE:- The New Guard

Chapter 8 - Never trust a German sausage!

Fredrick the German spy had acquired all the equipment he needed for his escape to the German territory. Fredrick had entered a local hospital facility then stole the uniform and papers of an injured English officer then returned to his safe house with the help of some local French / German sympathisers, what he didn't realise one of them was a double agent a little wire hair haired Dachshund called Jaeger had been relaying information about his plan back to Dani De Marie in Amsterdam.

Fredrick sat in his room with the uniform and paper work laid out across his bed, he suddenly

CASE FILE:- The New Guard

thought he had better check the precious package he had in his possession as it had been out of his sight for too long. He felt down the side of his bed next to the bedroom wall and pulled out an old leather briefcase, then opened it. Yes it was still there, he had no idea what it must be, but it must be very important as both Generals Rommel and Maximilian heads of German Intelligence had ordered him to intercept the SDS operative then return with his belongings directly to them. Fredrick looked at the object and not for one second did he realise the power he held in his paw!

CASE FILE:- The New Guard

After some alterations to the uniform and a slight change to some of the paperwork Fredrick was ready to go. The local sympathisers had acquired a motorbike for him to use and so he set off to Saissons.

The journey wasn't easy for him as there were more and more check points the nearer he got to the frontline, but due to his cunning disguise he went through without too much hassle. He carried on until he reached his last check point and the front line, it was becoming dark and he needed to find somewhere to hold up until he could put his next part of the plan in to action.

CASE FILE:- The New Guard

That night he found a dug out in trench wall and settled himself down for the night, when out of nowhere the sounds of machine gun fire made him awoke with a start. He looked around and could see soldiers rushing over the trenches and entering in to no man's land.

The gun fire carried on for another 20 minutes and then fell an eerily silence. Fredrick looked about and found a periscope to be able to look over the

CASE FILE:- The New Guard

trench wall. The sight that he saw chilled him to the bone, he knew they were the enemy that had been killed, but he couldn't stop the feeling of deep regret of such a waste of life. He laid the periscope down beside him and closed his eyes trying his best to rid his mind of such horror.

The morning was cool when he finally awoke he had, had a troubled sleep and after the sight of that nights horror had reinforced his decision not to try and cross the front line that way by going over the battlefield. He took his time to find out where and what Regiment were doing what? He soon found the unit he was looking for, it was an unit of Engineers who were specialists in tunnelling.

CASE FILE:- The New Guard

The head of the unit was a Captain Jack Russell a small terrier but a specialist in digging. Serving under him was a Welsh Sealyham Terrier, a Sergeant Owen Lucas and a number of privates of which were terriers of different breeds.

Captain Jack Russell

Engineer

Breed: Jack Russell Terrier

Serial number: 24797

Gender: Male

Age: 5 years

CASE FILE:- The New Guard

Sergeant Owen Lucas

Engineer

Breed: Sealyham terrier

Serial number: 22794

Gender: Male

Age: 9 years

Fredrick approached the Captain and in his boldest manner then proceeded to tell the Captain that he now had orders from HQ to dig a tunnel at a point on the map he was pointing at in his paws, little did the Captain know that the Germans were busily digging from the opposite direction at the same point. The Captain looked at the map and at the freshly forged orders then called in his Sergeant, "Owen, we will be commencing a dig here, gather the

CASE FILE:- The New Guard

men and equipment" he ordered, "Yes sir, right away sir." Sergeant Lucas replied as he rushed off to gather the men. Fredrick retained his composure, but inside he was delighted as his plan was falling in to place.

Sergeant Lucas was on the case the men had been gathered and the Engineers were busily excavating the side of the trench wall. Fredrick asked the Sergeant how long did he think it would take them to reach the other side, the Sergeant had thought approximately 4 days. So as the German Engineers were digging from opposite end that time should be halved, great he thought, all he could do now is sit back and wait.

CASE FILE:- The New Guard

Chapter 9 - The tale of two tunnels.

Dutch and Bentley had left the Inn early as they were pushed for time. They carried on along the Allied line until they approached their destination. They were then stopped by French troupes led by a Major Chanttelle LeChamp a Beauceron with an imposing physique.

Major Chanttelle Lechamp.

French Army Reserves

Breed: Beauceron

Serial number: 23798-25

Gender: Female

Age: 7 years

CASE FILE:- The New Guard

"Sorry Gentlemen you cannot take this route." The major informed them, after a short discussion and complimenting them on their magnificent moustaches, they had found out the Germans had advanced on that point in the line and it was too dangerous for them to travel upon that route. Dutch looked at the map and decided to take a route over an adjacent hill and work their way around. As the Morgan reached the top of the Hill our two heroes looked out over the area in which they were going to drive and saw themselves the magnitude of the conflict.

CASE FILE:- The New Guard

Dutch's thoughts turned to Kevin and were hoping that he wasn't in the middle of that Battle. "I hope Kevin is not down there!" Dutch said out loud. "I'm sure he's not, I bet he's safe and sound in a tent somewhere." Replied Bentley; trying not to worry about it himself. They pressed on and soon arrived on the other side of Saissons, they pulled up the car and looked around it was a hive of activity with troops running backwards and forwards obviously

CASE FILE:- The New Guard

following their orders. Dutch grabbed the attention of a passing soldier and asked where the command HQ was, they then made their way to the HQ to speak to the Commanding Officer for their help to track down Fredrick the spy.

They introduced themselves to the commanding officer a General Winston Marlborough an old English Mastiff who was stuck in his ways, who immediately when introducing themselves took little notice of the two them, that is until they showed their Watch Dog Division IDs, his face and attitude changed from that point on, he couldn't be more helpful if he tried. The General called for all his officers to meet at the HQ immediately.

CASE FILE:- The New Guard

All the officers met at the HQ except for Captain Russell.

Captain Russell was busy supervising the tunnel being dug by his troops who were making record time as they were just reaching the halfway mark.

Back at HQ the discovery of Captain Russell's absence hadn't gone amiss. Dutch questioned the Captains last where about then made off withBentley in tow in case his suspicions were right!

Sergeant Lucas was the first to hear what he thought was scratching coming from the tunnel face. He ordered his men to stop and he listened for a

CASE FILE:- The New Guard

few seconds, he couldn't hear anything this time, so ordered them back to work. Strange he thought to himself, I better go and check with Captain Russell in case on the Geological map it shows an underground stream or something nearby? So off he went to speak to the Captain.

The Captain wasn't alone, the strange looking officer aka Fredrick was with him as he had been for the last few hours. Sergeant Lucas discussed the situation with the Captain when Fredrick announced he would go and confirm the Sergeants concerns, that in his old leather briefcase he had with him was state of the art vibration detectors in which would give them an answer and off he went

CASE FILE:- The New Guard

down the tunnel. Fredrick approached the tunnel wall trying not to smile as he knew exactly what the noise was and so would the troop digging in front of him soon enough.

The last thing the troop of Terriers knew was all of a sudden the Tunnel face collapsed on top of them and the voices of German Dachshunds now entering their tunnel!

The Terriers were disorientated and caught by surprise all they could see and hear through the commotion was Fredrick speaking German and heading off down the German side of the tunnel. Before they could gather their thoughts enough to give chase along the tunnel there was a huge

CASE FILE:- The New Guard

explosion from the German side of the tunnel. The tunnel shook with the force, the noise was deafening and the air had turned in to a cloud full of dust.

Captain Russell, pulled out his officers whistle and started to blow for assistance, as he and Sergeant Lucas rushed in to the tunnel looking for survivors.

Dutch and Bentley heard the explosion as they were heading towards the tunnel and picked up their pace. As they approached the tunnel entrance initially there was an eerie silence and then a few moments later the sounds of faint coughing then the cry of troops in pain could be heard.

CASE FILE:- The New Guard

They both rushed in to the tunnel to help and started to carry the injured out to the surface.

Finally everyone was accounted for and by some miracle no fatalities. The Terriers were shell shocked, bruised and battered, but they were sturdy little dogs and would soon be back in to service.

Dutch approached Captain Russell and showed the Captain a picture of Fredrick the spy and asked "Was this officer in the tunnel with you Captain?" The Captain replied "Yes Sir!" He then panicked and ordered Sergeant Lucas to carry on the search for the missing officer.

CASE FILE:- The New Guard

Dutch, Bentley and the Sergeant headed back in to the tunnel, when one of the privates stopped them in their tracks and told them what had happened.

No thought Dutch, he then ordered Bentley and asked the Sergeant to do a full sweep of the tunnel just in case Fredrick had dropped the time collar as he was trying to escape? After a short while, both Bentley and the sergeant emerged empty handed.

"Bentley we are going to have to travel across to the other side of the line!" Dutch informed him. "We're not taking the Morgan are we?"

Bentley replied. "NO, no, we're going to have to commandeer a biplane from the C.A.F." said Dutch.

CASE FILE:- The New Guard

It took them a while to commandeer a biplane that wasn't in immediate use and the only one they could use was being patched together due to bullet holes through the wings!

Bentley looked at the Biplane then turned to Dutch with an amazing bit of self control he proceeded to tell Dutch his thoughts of going up in the air in a Biplane full of bullet holes and that it maybe not the best thing to do! Dutch reassured him, he also pointed out this was the only Biplane

CASE FILE:- The New Guard

available and they needed to catch up to that spy before it was too late! Bentley knew he had to do it for the mission's sake and so steeled himself and climbed in to the cock pit.

Everything was going Okay until a mechanic that was starting the Biplane wished them good luck and to be aware that the Brown Baron was in the area! Oh no not the Brown Baron, thought Bentley! The Brown Baron had gained his reputation as an Ace fighter pilot early in the war due to all the Allied Biplanes he had shot down!

CASE FILE:- The New Guard

C.A.F Report

Brown Baron - Manfred von Woofthofen

Brown Barons Tri-plane identified as a Fokker DR.I.

Before Bentley could think twice, Dutch opened up the throttle on the Biplane and was speeding along the runway and taking off towards the German held territory.

"Keep your eyes open for enemy planes!" Dutch ordered Bentley. There was no need to ask Bentley twice, his head was swivelling about trying to see in all directions at once.

They passed over the top of no man's land between the two opposing armies and could not believe the

CASE FILE:- The New Guard

level of destruction below them, what were once beautiful farmed fields were now covered in mud, huge craters from the Artillery shells and barbed wire for as far as the eye could see.

As they flew closer to the German lines they came under gun fire from the troops below. Bentley was mentally willing Dutch to raise the Biplane out of range of the guns as he sat there watching more bullet holes appearing around him in the Biplanes fuselage and wings. Bentley looked about the cock pit to see if there was anything to protect himself with?

CASE FILE:- The New Guard

At Bentleys feet was a canvas bag and so he peered inside of it. He immediately started to sneeze and drew his head back out of the bag. He shouted to Dutch and asked what the Biplane had been used for before they commandeered it? Dutch replied that the Biplane had been used for a vital stock run for the canteen and why did he ask? "Oh nothing" Bentley replied as he proceeded to empty the canvas bag over the German troops, which certainly stopped them from shooting at them for awhile.

CASE FILE:- The New Guard

Damn Bentley thought, I wish I had my car horn with me I could've poop pooped them as well he chuckled. Dutch scanned the Landscape and then back to the map he had with him, he was guessing the tunnel that the Germans had dug would be in straight line to intercept theirs, so needed a place to land as close as he could to where he thought the tunnel entrance might be.

He found a perfect spot behind some woodland nearby and with Bentleys help landed the plane then hid it, hopefully to keep it from arousing suspicion from the patrolling German troops.

"Okay Bentley I think that's enough!" Dutch ordered, as Bentley was kicking further amounts of

CASE FILE:- The New Guard

grass and soil over the plane. "We're camouflaging a Biplane, not burying a bone!" Dutch instructed. "Okay, Okay, but you can never be too careful." replied Bentley, Dutch argued "But how many bones have you lost in the process?" "Fair point." Bentley answered. The pair of them approached the edge of the woods then stopped to survey the area. The remains of the tunnel could be seen but no Fredrick the spy in sight. They needed information and fast! Bentley noticed a lone sentry near the tunnel remains then pointed them out to Dutch. "Okay, we need to interrogate that sentry Bentley, any ideas?" Dutch asked. Bentley thought for a second or so, "I have a bone in my rucksack; we can creep up and smack them on the head with it!"

CASE FILE:- The New Guard

Replied Bentley, Dutch looked at him and answered "First of all, why have you brought a bone on to a mission? Secondly, how can we question them if you knock them out?" Bentley didn't reply, but it did give Dutch time to think of a plan and Bentley may not like it. Dutch explained to Bentley that the bone would be pivotal to the plan and to trust him. Bentley went along with it begrudgingly.

The sentry was thinking to themselves what an unusual day it had been, one minute it had been quiet, then a large explosion and a British officer running with some officers speaking German towards the German HQ, strange? Just as he thought strange, out of the corner of his eye he caught the

CASE FILE:- The New Guard

glimpse of something in the bushes? He went over to investigate. He looked through the bushes and he was sure he kept seeing something there just out of reach each time he moved forward until he made his way in to a small clearing. There in front of him was a large bone, he couldn't help himself he had to have a chew on it, his mind was so preoccupied on chewing he hadn't even noticed the string attached to the bone, when all of a sudden out of nowhere a smelly, upset Bulldogge grabbed him and started to twist his ears! The next thing he knew a small dashing terrier with a magnificent moustache was questioning him about the strange British officer he had seen earlier. "Talk or my good friend will twist your ears off!" Dutch ordered the frightened

CASE FILE:- The New Guard

sentry. "All I know the British officer went off to HQ carrying a brief case with him." replied the sentry. Dutch looked at Bentley and nodded. Bentley proceeded to use Bentleys bone as a gag by tying it in to place and hogtied the sentry. Bentley all the way through Dutch's actions just kept pulling faces at the thought he would not see that bone again!

The two of them left the sentry tied up in the bushes and made their way back to the Biplane. Dutch knew the spy had a head start, but he was making his way by road and they were taking to the air again.

"The German HQ is 12 miles in that direction" Dutch told Bentley as pointed North East after

CASE FILE:- The New Guard

studying the map they had. There was no response, "Bentley are you listening?" Dutch asked, still no response. "Okay I'm sorry I sacrificed your bone." said an apologetic Dutch. "Hmm, Okay. But I was really looking forward to that one." replied Bentley still sulking. "Come on keep focused on what's important." Dutch reminded him. "It was important to me" Bentley quietly answered as he climbed in to the cockpit of their Biplane then took off.

CASE FILE:- The New Guard

Chapter 10 .... The German HQ, end of the line?

Fredrick Dewurst arrived at HQ so immediately made contact to General Rommel and Maximilian via telegraph using Morse code. The Generals response was to remain where he was and that they would come to him personally. Fredrick had never felt so important, two high commanding Generals coming to him, as he walked off to the canteen for a lunch of Bratwurst and sauerkraut.

Dutch and Bentley were approximately 4 miles from the German HQ when all of a sudden, bang, bang, bang, bang, bang, rip! Quickly Bentley

CASE FILE:- The New Guard

spotted an Enemy aircraft bearing down on them and had started to shoot at them. Bentley shouted to Dutch who was flying, 9 o'clock high! Dutch knew what Bentley meant, that the enemy Biplane was attacking from that direction! Dutch swung the plane around trying to miss the gunfire. "Bentley man the machine gun!" Dutch cried to Bentley. Bentley turned around and cockled the machine gun at the back of the Biplane and started to scan for the enemy Biplane again. Bang, bang, bang, they were being shot at again! "Can you see the Biplane Bentley?" Dutch asked. Oh Bentley had seen the Biplane and was struck with terror as he recognised the Biplanes markings, it was their worst

CASE FILE:- The New Guard

nightmare it was the Brown Baron Manfred von Woofthofen! Bentley was finally able to answer in a very frightened and squeaky voice " Brown Baron! Brown Baron! It's the Brown Baron!" Dutch took control of the situation and tried to reassure Bentley as best as he could as well as dodge the hail of Bullets that were being fired in their direction. Dutch dodged and weaved the Biplane with no effect as the Brown Baron carried on his pursuit until Bentley could see The Baron looking straight down his gun sights aimed at him and Dutch! Bentley in panic turned and grabbed Dutch trying to hug him hanging half out of his cockpit shouting "We're going to die!" hysterically. As Bentley grabbed Dutch and pulled him in to hug him the

CASE FILE:- The New Guard

knock on effect was that Dutch was still holding the planes controls and as Bentley pulled, the Biplane suddenly flew erratically straight up and then in to a loop!

From the Brown Barons point of view he thought he had them, the last thing he knew was that he was looking down the gun sights when he saw a chubby Bulldogge that looked like it was trying to climb in to the front cockpit, then all of a sudden the biplane steeply climbed and rolled over in to a loop. The Brown Baron looked up to find out where the enemy Biplane was and the next he knew the world had gone black and there was an awful stench! His lack of vision caused the Baron to

CASE FILE:- The New Guard

crash land his Tri-plane and after realising what had made him crash has never come forward with the true account of his accident.

Dutch had been struggling with Bentley until he smelt something and cried "Bentley you haven't!?" Bentley sat back in his seat, embarrassed and apologised "I'm sorry, I couldn't help it, I was scared and you know I have problems down there" referring to his bowel. Dutch looked about for the pursuing Baron who was not immediately to sight? He turned the Biplane around to see what had happened, then noticed the Baron's Tri-plane in a field with a figure waving obscenities at them!

CASE FILE:- The New Guard

"Bentley I'm not sure what just happened, but I think luck was on our side?" Dutch informed Bentley.

Bentley looked at the sight of the Baron in distress then it dawned on him what might have happened! Oops! He thought to himself, oh well that will teach you, as he carried on chuckling to himself.

Dutch adjusted the Biplane back on course and off they went, desperately trying to regain the time they had just lost due to the Brown Barons attack.

Dutch brought the Biplane down and tried to Camouflage it the best they could, but it still stuck out in the surrounding landscape, they had no

CASE FILE:- The New Guard

choice so had to take a chance that no one would find it to be able to escape back to the allied lines.

From their Biplane to the HQ was approximately a mile of heavily guarded German troops. Dutch scanned the map and it was agreed they had to wait until night fell to aid them from detection. Dutch looked about to look for anything that would help conceal them as they made their attempt to enter the HQ. There was a stream nearby so Dutch made his way down to the bank then pointed at the wet oozing mud, "If we roll in this mud it will help camouflage us from the German troops, they won't be able to see us!" Dutch informed Bentley.

CASE FILE:- The New Guard

"What? You want me to roll in that muck. Nope, No way! It could be a sewage outlet for all you know?" replied Bentley. Dutch scooped up some of the mud and sniffed, "No it's fine!" Dutch answered then proceeded to roll in it backwards and forwards until he was covered from head to tail. "You seem to be enjoying that more than you should?" Bentley said in disgust. "Its fine, it's great for your skin!" replied Dutch. "Hmm, I'm still not doing it." Bentley answered. Dutch was starting to become impatient with Bentley due to the fact that Bentley was predominantly white in colour and even though the darkness of night would help he would still stand out like a sore thumb. So Dutch had a think about it, Hmm how can I get Bentley to roll in the

CASE FILE:- The New Guard

mud? Then it dawned on him. Dutch proceeded to pick up a piece of mud and pretend to eat it. "Oh this is so yummy, I never realised that it tastes exactly like chocolate mousse!" The bait had been set and Bentley's ears twitched. "Yum, yum, oh this so good." Dutch carried on. All of a sudden Bentley launched himself face first in to the most sloppiest part of the muddy bank, with his mouth open all he could think of this mountain of goodness in front of him that he was never allowed to have, because Kevin his master had said chocolate was poisonous to dogs. He rolled around for a few minutes eating mouthfuls of dirt and mud when he suddenly announced "Chocolate mousse tastes horrible!" as he spat the remainder of the mud from his mouth.

CASE FILE:- The New Guard

Dutch tried to look surprised and held himself back from laughing then answered "Shame, obviously Kevin was right not to let you have it in the past." Bentley quickly replied "but you enjoyed it?" Dutch replied "My mistake it was a beetle that I was crunching on" as he smiled to himself and thought at least Bentley is a bit safer now he's camouflaged.

Night fell and our unlikely heroes made their way to the HQ.

German Head Quarters

Location- German occupied territory approximately 12 miles North East of the town of Saissons.

CASE FILE:- The New Guard

Apart from a few near misses their concealed advancement across the last mile to the HQ worked. Our heroes entered the HQ and went about searching for Fredrick the spy.

Fredrick had just taken arrival of the Generals who he had left to be entertained in the briefing room whilst he went off to fetch his briefcase from the room he had been using during his brief visit.

As Dutch and Bentley were creeping through the corridors of the HQ they stopped abruptly due to the sound of hurried footsteps approaching. They concealed themselves within the shadows and watched as a figure approached. It was Fredrick and he was carrying a briefcase!

CASE FILE:- The New Guard

Fredrick had no clue the SDS operators were there, it was the last thing on his mind; all he was concerned about was handing over the contents of his briefcase and looking forward to the praise and honours that may be bestowed upon him.

Bentley sprang and grabbed Fredrick in a vice like grip then threw Fredrick to the ground. Dutch galvanised in to action by making Fredrick release his grip of the brief case. Fredrick tried to raise the alarm by howling, But Bentley had anticipated him doing that by clamping Fredrick's mouth shut with his paw. Dutch quickly looked inside the brief case and there was the late Watch Dog operator's time collar still in one piece. Dutch nodded to

CASE FILE:- The New Guard

Bentley to acknowledge the collar was there. Bentley then asked Dutch what they were going to do with Fredrick? Fredrick was thinking the worst so started to struggle for what he thought was for his life. Dutch thought it over, after all the death and destruction they had seen recently he couldn't bring himself to order Bentley to end Fredrick. Fredrick could sense the struggle Dutch was having in making a decision so just waited for the right moment. Dutch looked at Bentley and said "We can't kill him Bentley! If anything of this war that is going on around us has taught me is that life is precious, we can't just kill him." Bentley looked Dutch in the eyes then replied "My friend, I'm glad you said that as I couldn't do it." Bentley looked

CASE FILE:- The New Guard

down, there was Fredrick doing the perfect sad face, ears drooping, large puppy eyes, whimpering and really looking sorry for himself. Bentley immediately felt sorry for him so released his grip slightly, with that Fredrick took his chance, he wriggled and squirmed like no sausage dog had done before! Bentley was trying his hardest to retain his grip but to no avail, Fredrick had got loose! Fredrick ran down the corridors howling an alarm call, then turned back at his pursers and taunted them "Suckers!" as he carried on racing away towards the direction of the noise of hurried footsteps from troops approaching their position. Bentley came to a standstill, "Quick through here." Bentley shouted to Dutch. Dutch stopped and looked

CASE FILE:- The New Guard

back to an entrance to another corridor which Bentley was entering. Dutch turned around, and then caught up with Bentley. "What next?" asked Dutch. Bentley hadn't thought that far ahead so was desperately scanning the way ahead looking for an exit that they could use.

Fredrick had intercepted the guards so directed them towards the corridor that our two heroes had entered. Then Fredrick carried on towards the briefing room to which the Generals were waiting. Fredrick entered the room and there waiting for him impatiently was General Maximilian Rottwiel and his brother General Rommel. They stood their eyeing Fredrick up and down as he entered the

CASE FILE:- The New Guard

room, they could tell something was wrong. "Um, Um. Evening Generals." Fredrick nervously announced. Then stood there patiently awaiting their response whilst admiring their chains of rank and office that hung around there necks. General Rommel was the first to reply in a deep, dominating voice, "So where is our package that you promised us?" Fredrick nervously looked up, down, anywhere other than the direction of the two Generals. "That's the funny thing," Fredrick replied. The Generals stepped forward and were now towering over the top of Fredrick. "Carry on!" General Maximilian ordered. Fredrick's knees started to wobble as he answered" The funny thing is that I had your item and two SDS operatives have it now."

CASE FILE:- The New Guard

Fredrick closed his eyes anticipating the worst. General Rommel crouched down to quietly speak in to Fredrick's ear "So where are the operatives then?" "Oh their still in the HQ, well they were the last time I saw them." Fredrick replied. General Rommel closed his eyes then took a deep breath, "instead of just standing there, take us to where you last saw them!" he ordered. Fredrick didn't even respond he could see the anger in the Generals face which was matched by his brother Maximilian. Fredrick turned on his heels and quickly made off to the last place he had seen the two operatives with the two Generals hot on his heels.

CASE FILE:- The New Guard

C.I.9 intelligence report

General Rommel Rottweil

Country- German

Sex- Male

Age - Unknown

Serial number - Unknown

C.I.9 intelligence report

General Maximilian Rottweil

Country - German

Sex - Male

Age - unknown

Serial number - Unknown

CASE FILE:- The New Guard

There was bedlam within the HQ with troops running backwards and forwards searching for Dutch and Bentley.

Bentley had opened a door to a communal bathroom; in the bathroom was a long row of toilet seats in which sat on top of a long box with no divisions between each toilet seat. Dutch scanned around the room a dead end! "So where now?" Dutch questioned Bentley. "Umm." Bentley was raking his brain trying to think what to do next? "I've got it!" Bentley replied as his eyes gazed upon the toilets. Dutch looked at him almost willing him to just answer. Bentley carried on "The toilets!" "What you're going to make some sort of methane bomb, so

CASE FILE:- The New Guard

we can escape?" asked Dutch. Now Bentley hadn't thought of that idea but they were desperately running out of time! "Not exactly." answered Bentley, "What do you mean not exactly?" "You're not thinking, what I think your thinking of!" "No!" protested Dutch before Bentley could even say a word. "We have no choice Dutch, if we don't do something in the next minute we're done for!" Bentley reminded him. "But, But, no not there!" Dutch pleaded. "No choice!" As Bentley lifted the toilet seat, held his nose then jumped in to the toilet box! Dutch felt his pride leave him as he followed suit and jumped in the toilet beside Bentleys. At first Dutch didn't want to open his

CASE FILE:- The New Guard

eyes to the horror of his surroundings. But after a short while he opened his eyes to check on Bentley.

Bentley had immediately regretted his decision so trying not to vomit on himself due to the stench he was sitting in he was about to raise the toilet lid to climb back out when the door of the bathroom opened. Dutch looked at Bentley; Bentley looked at Dutch as they could hear the footsteps get closer and closer to the toilets! They then heard two guards talking and acknowledged that Dutch and Bentley were not in the room. Both our heroes sighed with a relief, when suddenly one of the guards said he would catch up in a minute. Both our heroes sat as quiet as mice when suddenly the lid

CASE FILE:- The New Guard

on Bentley's toilet opened, then that's when Bentley felt a warm wet sensation running down his neck! Bentley started to try and move but with no luck and was about to say something when Dutch placed his paw over his mouth to stop him. The next 3 minutes felt like a life time to Bentley until the guard had finished his business then left the bathroom. Bentley slowly raised his head from the toilet and scanned the room, the room was clear so he proceeded to climb his way out of the toilet, Dutch noticed Bentley's actions so followed suit.

Bentley stopped then looked at himself in a bathroom the sight made him shudder in disgust in what he was covered in. "I don't know why you're

CASE FILE:- The New Guard

pulling those faces?" Dutch snapped at him, "It was your idea to jump in there!" Dutch carried on. Bentley just whimpered "But I'm covered, I'm covered..." "In poop."

Dutch finished his sentence. "But, but!" Bentley was trying to reply. "Anyway I thought you were use to it; I mean you do have Colitis!" Dutch snapped again. "Yes, but I don't roll in it!" Bentley said defensively. Dutch stood back for a second and looked at his friends discomfort about the subject. "I'm sorry Bentley that was wrong of me to say that, I know it must be embarrassing for you." Dutch apologised. Bentley replied "It's Ok, I know you didn't mean it." then opened up for hug.

CASE FILE:- The New Guard

Dutch looked at him and responded "No way! You stink!" Bentleys face broke in to a smile, then he started to chuckle as the pair laughed at their situation, but it wasn't for long as Dutch brought their minds back to the situation at hand.

"I think the only way out is, back up the corridor we came from, as my thoughts are that the guards have already checked this area so it should be safer." Dutch relayed to Bentley. Bentley agreed, so they made off back down the corridor where they originally came from.

Fredrick was still trailing behind the two Generals as they reached the corridor where he had last seen the SDS operatives. "The corridor on your

CASE FILE:- The New Guard

right" instructed Fredrick. The two Generals turned the corner still running and the next thing they knew they had collided with two dogs running the opposite way. Dutch went flying due to his size and hit the corridor wall with a thud and was dazed by the impact. Bentley had hit General Rommel with his head, straight in to Rommel's stomach; Bentley had lost his footing so causing him to slide on the polished floors through the Generals legs. Rommel was doubled up on the floor now trying to recover his wind after it had just been knocked out of him, when all of a sudden, he sniffed and sniffed again. "Ugh, poo! What's that smell!?" He then noticed the skid mark left by Bentley on the polished floor! "What is going on?" The General bellowed.

CASE FILE:- The New Guard

General Maximilian had already at that point grabbed Dutch by the scruff and was holding him out at arm's length, whilst using his other paw to cover his nose.

"It's them Generals, it's them!" Fredrick informed excitedly.

Before the Generals could react, Bentley rushed Maximilian. Maximilian saw what Bentley was covered in, panicked and let go of Dutch! "Run!" Bentley screamed to Dutch. Dutch didn't need to be told twice, he checked he still had the case and was up on his toes and off running, with Bentley close on his heels.

CASE FILE:- The New Guard

"Why did you let home go!?" Rommel barked at his brother. "Maximilian snapped back "Well I didn't see you step forward and do anything?" Whilst the two Generals were arguing Fredrick just stood there waiting to say something, then finally he found the courage to say something. "Hmm, Generals, Sirs, I think their getting away!" The two Generals stopped in midsentence and turned to look at Fredrick. Fredrick felt the courage that was there suddenly seep out through his legs as his knees started to knock in fear. "Maximilian's anger was still fresh as he barked at Fredrick," then why are you still standing here? Get after them!"

CASE FILE:- The New Guard

Fredrick ran off in the direction our heroes had taken, leaving the two Generals to follow him.

Rommel turned to his brother as they followed Fredrick a short distance behind and quietly said "If we don't recover that collar, the DR will want someone to pay for this mistake!" Maximilian glanced towards Fredrick and replied "I think that can be arranged." as he gestured towards Fredrick!

Bentley and Dutch had made it to the court yard where they had entered the HQ originally.

"Almost there!" Bentley said in anticipation. "HALT!!!" an order came from the shadows, then suddenly the court yard was illuminated as our heroes stood in the middle of the yard, they

CASE FILE:- The New Guard

quickly scanned the area, and the whole area was surrounded by guards armed to the teeth with guns.

Dutch looked at Bentley, then nodded as to say it's OK, then proceeded to raise his hands to surrender, in which a split second later Bentley did the same. As the guards came in to seize them Dutch whispered to Bentley "Don't worry, whatever happens I'm with you." The guards grabbed the pair of them and immediately started to protest due to the smell! The officer of the guards reinforced his order and threatened the guards if they did not do their duty properly over a bit of poop.

The next voice that was heard was one both our heroes had only just recently heard, Bentley's

CASE FILE:- The New Guard

stomach churned with nerves when he recognised it.

"Captain take those prisoners to the shower block, clean them up, then take them to the dungeon, so we can question them later!" General Rommel ordered.

Dutch and Bentley were marched off to await their outcome!

CASE FILE:- The New Guard

Chapter 11....... Weakness's can be our greatest strengths.

Our heroes sat in a damp, dank, poorly lit dungeon. Dutch asked Bentley "Are you Okay?" Bentley replied "Yeah I'm Okay, I just wish the water they had used on us had been warmer!" as he sat there shivering.

Dutch tried his restraints again, but all his paws were tightly buckled with leather straps. "Can you get out of your restraints?" Dutch asked. Bentley tried but with no success. "No, I'm not going anywhere!" replied Bentley. They suddenly heard footsteps; they waited as they came closer and

CASE FILE:- The New Guard

closer! A guard appeared checked the cell they were in and marched off again. The waiting seemed forever, they no longer knew if it was night or day. But through it all they tried to keep their spirits up between themselves by playing eye spy. "Ok my turn. Eye spy with my little eye something that starts with H." said Bentley. "H?" replied Dutch, "Yes H." Bentley answered. "Hmm, H." Dutch said to himself as he looked around the room. "You're not cheating again are you?" Dutch asked him. "No, no I'm not." Bentley replied. Dutch carried on scanning the room so becoming more and more frustrated. After a short while Dutch had to admit defeat, "Okay I'm done; you win what starts with H?" Bentley sat there with a smug look upon

CASE FILE:- The New Guard

his face and announced what it was "HQ." as he chuckled with glee as he had won. "No, No, you're cheating again!" Dutch argued. "I won, you didn't, so that's that." Bentley carried on smugly. "But you cheated!" Dutch replied. "Nope I won." Bentley carried on. "Oh you're so annoying!" Dutch answered as he started to sulk.

Whilst busily arguing between themselves they hadn't noticed they were no longer the only ones in the cell.

"Cough, cough. May be once you two have finished, we can get started?" Dutch and Bentley stopped bickering then turned to the direction of the voice. There was General Rommel and Maximilian, plus a very nervous Fredrick. The voice had been from

CASE FILE:- The New Guard

General Maximilian, once their attention had been caught he carried on in menacing tone, "I'm sorry to have kept you waiting for so long, but we have been awaiting for someone to arrive who has been waiting for this day for a very, very long time." Dutch and Bentley looked at each other then shrugged their shoulders puzzled by Maximilian's statement. As they were puzzling it over in their minds, the sound of uneven footsteps came closer and closer towards the entrance of the cell. Dutch was struggling to see this new figure, then suddenly the gas lights were turned up, there standing in between the two Generals was an old German Wire Haired Pointer with a damaged rear leg.

CASE FILE:- The New Guard

"Good day to you gentlemen. Let me introduce myself. I am DR Einer Steiner and you are my guests." The Doctor announced to our two heroes. Bentley responded "Ah good day dear Sir, are you the person to speak to about the room service here? I must complain, I haven't even seen a menu so far?" Dutch laughed. " Very amusing Captain Poopstacker, I'm sure you and Major Dude will take comfort in your humour after what we have planned for you." The Dr replied menacingly. Bentley stopped and so did Dutch then mouthed to each other "he knows our names?" The Dr carried on "Oh I know everything about you two!" Bentley gulped with fear. Dutch looked at him to reassure him and nodded to say he'll be Okay.

CASE FILE:- The New Guard

Over the next few hours the two SDS operators were subjected to countless bouts of torture and interrogation at the hands of Rommel and Maximilian. The hours past and still our plucky heroes would not talk as they knew that the fate of mankind was in their paws.

The Dr called a halt to the interrogation and ordered the two Generals to go and refresh themselves whilst he would have a chat with Dutch and Bentley.

The Generals left the Cell to refresh themselves so leaving just the three of them in the cell.

Dr Einer Steiner moved himself behind the two prisoners and lent down so they could hear

CASE FILE:- The New Guard

better. "Now, why would you go through all this suffering for a race such as humans? All they have ever done is enslaved us, treated us less than their own children! To add insult they keep those worthless creatures Cats! Cats I say! What have Cats ever done to benefit mankind, and we are treated the same as Cats!" The Dr ranted. Before either Dutch or Bentley could respond, the Dr carried on ranting "Well we will see how mankind fairs at the hands of D.I.S.T.E.M.P.E.R!" Dutch responded "Distemper that's a deadly disease for us dogs!" "Yes, yes and as deadly as it is to us, so our organisation DISTEMPER will be as deadly for Mankind!" The Dr replied and cackled.

CASE FILE:- The New Guard

"But you can't, the humans are our friends, we're here to look after them!" Bentley replied in concern.

<u>C.I.9 Intelligence report.</u>

<u>D.I.S.T.E.M.P.E.R</u>

Dogs. Intelligently. Seeking. Total. Elimination of. Mankind's. Power. Enslavement and. Rules

"Too late. I have the time collar that you were trying to retrieve. I just need the exact date

CASE FILE:- The New Guard

and time when your miserable organisation first started to protect the humans, so I can undo their meddling and allow mankind to destroy themselves!" The Dr informed them.

"I'd rather die, then tell you!" Dutch replied. He looked across to Bentley for back up. Bentley was mulling the idea over in his mind. "Bentley!" Dutch barked. "Oh, um, does it really need to be death?" Bentley asked. "Bentley!" Dutch snapped at him. "Okay, okay, if I have to. Yes over my dead body as well." Bentley finally answered.

The Dr waited a second before answering, "So be it. If you will not answer to reason I will have to use

CASE FILE:- The New Guard

the one thing you cannot resist!" Dutch replied with all the bravado he could muster, "Do your worst, we will never tell you!" The Dr took off his monocle and proceeded to clean it, then looked Dutch straight in to his eyes then said "I wasn't talking about you.." as he turned to face Bentley. Bentley gulped. "Don't you touch my friend." Dutch replied as he erupted into a fury as he struggled against his restraints.

The Dr stopped and turned towards the cell entrance then barked an order for Fredrick to come in. Fredrick looking sorry for himself ever since he was given the choice earlier by the Generals to

CASE FILE:- The New Guard

join DISTEMPER or face the consequences. He had no choice, all he ever wanted to do was to serve his country and to receive the respect he thought he deserved, now look at the mess he was in.

S.D.S Intelligence Report

Dr Einer Steiner

Head of D.I.S.T.E.M.P.E.R

Country: Unknown

Age: Unknown

Breed: German Wire haired Pointer

CASE FILE:- The New Guard

"Bring it here!" The Dr ordered, as Fredrick waddled across carrying a large silver platter with a lid on top. The Dr pointed to where he wanted Fredrick to leave the platter then dismissed him. Fredrick walked off thinking to himself, how am I going to get myself out of this mess?

Bentley's eyes were concentrating on the silver platter. What horrors lie underneath that lid he thought to himself?

DR Einer Steiner turned and slowly raised the lid and started to talk, "We have agents everywhere Captain Poopstacker there is nothing that is out of our reach!" With that he had exposed the one thing that could break Bentley! Dutch saw what was

CASE FILE:- The New Guard

there, "No, no it can't be!" Dutch cried out. "Yes, yes it is, our Agents obtained them all the way from England." "But, how?" Dutch asked. The Dr quickly replied "Our agents followed you on your training and found Bentleys Achilles heel! Greg the cook's sausage rolls from the canteen!" he laughed in torment. "No, Bentley!" Dutch cried. Bentley had already seen them; his mouth had fallen to one side as he started to dribble on himself, as he could imagine that succulent sausage meat and flaky pastry melting in his mouth. "Bentley please, no!" Dutch cried again, as Bentleys eyes had started too glaze over as he became more and more obsessed with the sight in front of him.

CASE FILE:- The New Guard

The Dr waved the sausage roll under Bentley's nose tickling his moustache on the way past, so gathering a few crumbs on its pass. His tongue shot out and licked up the crumbs, his senses immediately confirmed it was a Greg's sausage roll!

A tear appeared rolling down the side of Bentley's cheek due to the position he was in, he was stuck between duty and his instincts. The Dr carried on waving the sausage roll in front of him, repeating every few seconds what is the date and time coordinates? Dutch could see the punishment Bentley was going through then turned slightly in his direction and quietly said "Do what's right old

CASE FILE:- The New Guard

friend." Bentley composed his mind for a second, and then concentrated on Dutch, Kevin and his friends. He found the strength to resist. He started to pull on his restraints and then all of a sudden one leg was free! He quickly pulled the restraints off before the Dr had time to react. Bentley was now loose and bearing down on Einer Steiner. The startled Dr began to hobble toward the cells exit, when Bentley grabbed him and threw him with a perfect Shi-tsu throw. Before the Dr could recover Bentley used a Barkido chop and knocked him out. Bentley then turned to deal with the most important thing. "Bentley will you please let me out of these restraints, when you're not too busy eating all the sausage rolls?" Dutch enquired. "Oh,

CASE FILE:- The New Guard

oh yes sorry." Bentley mumbled with a sausage roll hanging out of his mouth. "So how did you escape?" Dutch asked. "Oh I turned my greatest weakness to my greatest strength." Bentley replied. Dutch carried on "What you were able to use your mental strength to break the bonds?" Bentley looked at him sheepishly "Not exactly! I dribbled on myself so much I was able to slip out of the bonds." He laughed. Dutch put a paw over his own eyes and replied "Oh Bentley."

"What now?" Bentley asked. "We must get that time collar back." said Dutch. "It would be so much easier if we could just go back in time and stop all this from happening in the first place!" replied

CASE FILE:- The New Guard

Bentley. Dutch looked at him and replied "You know what the Brigadier said, it is forbidden for us to use the collars to change the time lines for canines, and they are only used to protect mankind!" "But, but it would be so much simpler." Bentley argued. "I know, but we don't make the rules, there must be a reason behind it, this is also not the time to discuss it."

"So what do we do?" Bentley enquired again. Dutch thought through a plan. "Okay I've got it." Dutch replied and proceeded to explain his plan to him. Fredrick had been busily minding his own business trying his best to keep out of the two Generals sight, so he had remained near the dungeon.

CASE FILE:- The New Guard

"Fredrick!" "Fredrick, come here now!" he had heard from the direction of the cell. Oh no, what now? He thought to himself. Without questioning he raced off to the cell. When he arrived at the cell door he was too busy doing as he was told to notice anything wrong. He opened the door and rushed in busily asking "Yes sir, how can I help you?"

Fredrick saw two figures in the chairs and looked about the room, looking for the Dr. Then wallop; he was now face down on the floor!

"Sucker!" Bentley whispered in to Fredrick's ear. Fredrick thought to himself, it really isn't my day....

CASE FILE:- The New Guard

Dutch helped pick Fredrick up and then restrained him, then proceeded to ask him where was the time collar? After a bit of possession from Bentley, they found out the time collar was in the briefing room with the two generals. "So what do with him this time?" asked Bentley as looked at Fredrick. Dutch gestured to the chairs. "Really? After what he put us through." Bentley questioned. "It doesn't matter Bentley, we're still alive and he'll get his just deserts sooner or later." Dutch answered. "Okay, if you say so." Bentley said begrudgingly.

Once the Dr and Fredrick were secure in their restraints, Bentley had with delight stuffed his

CASE FILE:- The New Guard

old dirty handkerchief in to Fredrick's mouth to gag him, they were off to retrieve the collar.

They had quickly realised it must be early in the morning due to the lack of guards, so with their training put to good use made their way to the briefing room. They waited a short while to assess the situation. Both Generals had grown tired of waiting and made themselves comfortable in some wingback chairs in the briefing room. After a while they had both fallen asleep. The door creaked and Dutch eased it open very, very slowly, anticipating that he may well have to fight for his life at any second. The door was opened enough for him to ease his head through to take a sneaky look.

CASE FILE:- The New Guard

In the dull light from the gas lamps he scanned the room, but didn't see the two Generals immediately. He eased more of himself in to the room still scanning around. Then he noticed them asleep, he stopped to fix his bearings on where was the time collar? Ah on the table in the middle of the room! Dutch gestured to Bentley to stay where he was and to keep a look out, and then entered the room. Dutch tip toed across the briefing room floor until he reached the table where the time collar sat. Dutch nervously kept an eye on the now snoring Generals for a hint of movement. Maximilian snorted in his sleep; Dutch froze to the spot, his stomach doing cart wheels with nerves. He waited, wishing for Maximilian's eyes lids to

CASE FILE:- The New Guard

remain shut. Just as Dutch was about to turn back to make his escape, Maximilian's shoulders relaxed again, he was back in to a deep sleep.

Dutch wiped his brow with the back of his paw and let out a sigh of relief.

Bentley was watching the whole scene from the door way and his nerves were getting the better of him as he watched his friend dicing with peril. He watched as Dutch slowly picked up the time collar, and then turned towards the door to make his escape.

It was at this point Bentleys Colitis made its self known due to the stress he had been under. It started with a gurgle, then a rumble in his stomach

CASE FILE:- The New Guard

as he could feel his stomach expand! OH No Not Now! He thought. Bentley's eyes widened with panic as he gestured to Dutch to move quicker!

Dutch could see the panic on Bentleys face, but he didn't expect what would happen next.

Bentley in a panic looked around him; beside the door was a large vase full of cut flowers. He grabbed the vase, tossed out the flowers and sat on the vase.

With an almighty eruption the colitis let loose upon the vase!

Dutch stood there his jaw dropped with shock at the sight of Bentley on the vase; the sight for him was

CASE FILE:- The New Guard

surreal. The noise of Bentley's explosive colitis hadn't gone unnoticed as the sound had disturbed both Generals from their sleep with a start. As they awoke all they could see was Dutch hurrying towards the door with the collar and a strange Bulldogge doing something nasty in a vase! Rommel slapped himself in the face to make sure he wasn't still asleep, then turned to his brother for confirmation that what he saw was actually happening? Maximilian stared back at Rommel also looking shocked and bemused at the sight in front of them. Once realizing that what they saw was real, they leapt from their chairs to apprehend the two operatives.

CASE FILE:- The New Guard

Dutch came rushing through the door and slammed it behind him, then tried to find something to secure it shut. He looked about for something to use such as a bit of rope to tie the handle shut or a wedge of some type?

"Bentley, could you try and find something to secure the door?" Dutch asked as he held on to the door knob for dear life. "Yeah be right with you." Bentley replied then stepped off of the vase. Dutch had thought the sound was bad enough, but the stench was ten times worse coming from the vase, as he tried to hold on to the contents of his stomach. "Bentley, will you please look!" Dutch begged. "I'm on it, I'm on it!" Bentley replied. Bentley searched

CASE FILE:- The New Guard

about but nothing came to hand immediately, then it dawned on him, the large vase! He took the large vase and manoeuvred it closer to where Dutch was. Dutch moved away as much as he could without letting go of the door handle, with one quick sleight of hand, Bentley wedged the vase under the handle to secure it. Both Bentley and Dutch stood back to see if it would hold? Which it did at the annoyance to the two Generals cost.

"Let's go." Dutch ordered and off they went with the sounds of the Generals calling for help becoming fainter in the background as they made progress towards the court yard. A guard ran towards the briefing room door drawn by the sound

CASE FILE:- The New Guard

of the cries for help. As he approached he could hear the two Generals yelling to be let out, he approached the door to remove the vase when the stench hit him, he stood back and looked at it in disgust as he held his nose. "Let us out!" the Generals yelled. The guard looked at the vase and the contents; his mind was made up, as he nonchalantly walked off down the corridor in a different direction.

"Guard, Guard we know you're out there, open this door! That is an order!" General Rommel yelled as he could hear the sound of footsteps walking off down the corridor.

CASE FILE:- The New Guard

Whilst all this was happening a guard on his rounds had made the discovery of the Dr and Fredrick tied up inside the cell.

"Get me out of this chair!" the Dr ordered with anger in his voice. The guard hurriedly released the Dr, "I should leave you in that contraption after your stupidity." the Dr told a worried Fredrick. The guard paused from releasing Fredrick and waited on the Drs next move. The Dr thought and then ordered "Release him, I might have use for him." Fredrick was relieved, but at the same time concerned at the thought of what the Dr might have planned. The Dr

CASE FILE:- The New Guard

turned to Fredrick then ordered "Quick to the briefing room, they must not have that collar!" Fredrick didn't need to be told twice he and the guard raced off towards the briefing room.

As Fredrick raced towards the briefing room door, the louder he could hear the Generals cries to be let out. He noticed the vase wedged under the door handle and gestured to the guard for help to move it. The guard rushed forward took one whiff, then turned on his heels and ran off clutching his mouth. Fredrick held back his gag reflex and peered over the top of the vase to find out what was causing such horrendous stench? Oh my god! What

CASE FILE:- The New Guard

sort of monster would do such a thing? He thought to himself in shock. "I know you're out there, open this door now or I'll have your hide!" yelled General Maximilian.

Fredrick looked at the vase and mulled over the threats that were coming from the other side of the door, and then shuddered. He leant forward and with all his might he slowly eased the vase away from the door handle. The sudden release of pressure was noticed by the generals as they rammed the door open, to which in turn knocked the vase over on to a poor startled Fredrick! The Generals rushed out in to the corridor puzzled at the lack of a rescuer in sight? "Help, Help, Help."

CASE FILE:- The New Guard

came the muffled cries from an upturned vase. The two Generals looked at each other puzzled at the sight of a talking vase?

Rommel and Maximilian slowly raised the vase and out slid Fredrick covered in nastiness! As soon as Fredrick was free they dropped the vase again and immediately covered their noses. Rommel was the first to speak "Poo, that is nasty!" Fredrick just sat there not knowing what to do next and was close to tears. Maximilian spoke up whilst taking two to three steps backwards "Just go will you and clean yourself up!" Fredrick took his leave and slowly walked off to the showers trying not to slip on his way.

CASE FILE:- The New Guard

The two Generals headed off in the opposite direction to intercept the Dr to find out what they should do next?

CASE FILE:- The New Guard

Chapter 12..... Freedom is not at any cost.

The only transport our two heroes could find to make their escape was a couple of penny farthing bicycles. Dutch struggled to reach the pedals due to his shortness in leg length, but at least the HQ was on high ground. Bentley quickly opened the gates once the sentries had passed. Bentley turned to help Dutch to stabilise him, then gave him a mighty push towards freedom. Off went Dutch like a rocket, pedals spinning around and around wildly out of control. Bentley climbed up on to his Penny farthing then peddled like mad to catch up with his fast now disappearing friend! Bentley peddled away

CASE FILE:- The New Guard

and finally caught up with Dutch, who was busily hanging on for dear life.. "Wee, this is great!" said an over excited Bentley. Dutch daren't look at him in case he came off this horrid contraption. "Bentley will you be quiet!" replied Dutch. As Bentley peddled harder to make himself go faster. Bentley had seen a sentry at the end of the lane in the middle of the road busily doing his duty observing for incoming traffic approaching the HQ. Bentley grinned to himself as he tucked his head down to go faster as he approached the unknowing guard. Bentley positioned the Penny farthing to one side of the guard as he rode past he then kicked the guard in to the grass bank with a cry of "POOP, POOP!"

CASE FILE:- The New Guard

S.D.S Intelligence.

An artist impression of the Penny Farthings Major Dude and Captain Poopstacker made their escape from the HQ on.

The guard fell head first in to the grass bank and became stuck in the earth due to the large spike on top of his German pickelhaube helmet.

Dutch rushed past seconds later witnessing the guard trying their best to pull themselves from the bank.

CASE FILE:- The New Guard

As the lane went on, the gradient flattened off, so becoming level which had an effect on Dutch's progress, as he became slower and more unbalanced every few feet. "Bentley, stop!" Dutch yelled to grab his attention. Bentley eased the brakes on, then stepped off of his bicycle and looked around in the direction of Dutch. Dutch was wobbling side to side trying his best to stay on, but to no avail. With one misjudgement he came crashing down, with instinct from his Shi-tsu training he rolled his body away, free from harm. He stood up and dusted himself down then looked around to get his bearings. "The Biplane must be near?" he said to Bentley. "I think that woodland there is where we hid it." Bentley replied whilst gesturing towards a

CASE FILE:- The New Guard

wood a little way off from them. "Okay lets head in that direction." Dutch ordered.

As they approached the woodland they were suddenly knocked back by a huge explosion! "Oh no!" Bentley uttered. Their fears were confirmed the local troops had found their Biplane then proceeded to blow it up to foil their escape!

"What now?" Bentley asked. Dutch responded "We have no choice; we're going to have to get back to the German line, then somehow cross no man's land?"

Bentley felt sick to his stomach at the prospect of trying to cross that battlefield. Dutch was feeling the same. "Come on, we can't give in now, we've been through worse." as Dutch tried busily to build up

CASE FILE:- The New Guard

Bentleys sprit again. So off they went in the direction of the front line using all the cover to hand so not to be caught by the pursuing troops.

In the court yard of the HQ troops three forbidding figures walked towards an awaiting car. General Rommel opened the rear door to allow the Dr to enter the vehicle, while Maximilian menacingly spoke to Fredrick who was chauffeuring the car. "At least you smell a bit better than you did earlier!" He then turned and followed his brother in to the car. Fredrick sat there still damp from his shower and was steadily convinced he could still smell that nastiness still on him, as his nose wrinkled repulsed by the thought.

CASE FILE:- The New Guard

"Get a move on will you Fredrick, to the front line." The Dr ordered. Fredrick pulled the car through the HQ gates and roared off in the direction of the front line. Inside the back of the car the Dr sat there smiling to himself with the knowledge that he had telegraphed ahead to the front line troops to lay a trap for the two Watch Dog Operatives.

S.D.S Intelligence report.

Known DISTEMPER Automobile.

Make: Rolls Royce.

Model: Unknown

Distinctive crest on side of Automobile.

CASE FILE:- The New Guard

Dutch hid behind a tree stump to break up his outline from the enemy eye line. He looked out over the area and noticed an area where the barb wire was less stacked together, so looked like their only way in. They crept around until they were in line with the point that Dutch had noticed. They both quickly checked the area was free from enemy troops, and then made their move. Dutch rushed across to the barb wire fence and started to dig under it until he made a hollow in which he thought was big enough for him to crawl through. Dutch went down on his belly and crawled through commando style. Once he reached the other side he stopped to check the coast was clear. All Okay, so

CASE FILE:- The New Guard

he gave Bentley the thumbs up sign for Okay. Bentley got down and started to dig till he reached the size he thought he could fit through. Bentley copied Dutch then started to crawl through Commando style. "Ouch!" then again "Ouch!" came the muffled cries of Bentley, as he had grossly underestimated the size of his backside! Dutch couldn't help chuckling at the sight of Bentley slowly prying the barbs out of his bottom one by one. "Ouch, ouch, ouch!" as he pried the final one out, then made his way next to his friend rubbing the sore bits on the way. "Alright?" said Dutch sarcastically. "Hmmm..." Bentley answered with a look of displeasure. "There seems to be some sort of

CASE FILE:- The New Guard

storage area over there near the trenches, which will be our next point to reach." Dutch instructed.

Fredrick had made up lost time on the road due to the speed of the Rolls Royce and was soon entering the front line camp. An officer had come to greet them and became very subservient at the sight of the two Generals who exited the car. The officer proceeded to tell the Generals that his best troops were scouring the area and that the two operatives would not escape. It was at this point that Fredrick knew how the officer must of felt as General Rommel threatened the officer of the outcome if they weren't found. The officer's face turned a

CASE FILE:- The New Guard

pasty white as the colour drained from his face at the news of the threat.

The officer then turned and rushed off ordering any soldier nearby to do something.

The Dr leant forward from his seat and spoke in to Fredrick's ear slow and menacingly "Find me a map of this camp, now!" Fredrick hopped out of the car and rushed off after the officer to ask for a map.

The map showed the camp as whole, so the trenches were marked, Camp HQ and the storage area. The Dr looked over the map whilst sitting in the car still. He looked at all the scenarios in which would be easiest way to escape through to no man's land. The Dr had made his decision then said "There!" he

CASE FILE:- The New Guard

pointed at the storage area. He carried on saying "we will trap them there." "Rommel take some troops and make the barb wire more accessible at that point" as he pointed at the map. "Then hide a detachment of troops in the storage area out of sight, then wait. They will come to you!" "Maximilian you're with me."

Bentley was the first to reach the storage area and hid behind a crate waiting for Dutch to catch up. Bentley gestured that it was all clear, so Dutch moved in behind him. They both sat for a second or so to steady their nerves and to catch their breath. They sat there looking at area then realised that storage area was at the end of a trench line, that

CASE FILE:- The New Guard

if they could make their way across they might be able to go over the top on to the battle field.

"Ready?" Dutch asked Bentley. "Not yet, just give me a second." Bentley replied as he tried to settle his stomach, not wanting to go through what happened earlier. "Okay you take your time." Dutch replied reassuringly. Bentley took a few more seconds and he was ready, it was now or never. They both crept forward using each crate as camouflage to hide behind. They reached half way in to the storage area, when Dutch had an ill feeling come over him that something was wrong! "Bentley I don't like the look of this, I think it's a ....!" Before he could finish his sentence, cries of halt, stop where

CASE FILE:- The New Guard

you are! Came from all around them. Bentleys head whipped around in the directions of the voices. Dutch just looked down at the floor disappointed they had been caught. "What do we do?" asked Bentley panicking. Dutch slowly brought his head up to level again, but as his gaze followed the side of the box he noticed the German words that were stamped on the side of the box, Explosiv! He turned to Bentley and gestured to the crate. Bentley looked then also noticed the word, he nodded in response.

Dutch quickly pulled back the lid then pulled out the contents, hand grenades!! He gave some to Bentley and told him to throw them at the troops,

CASE FILE:- The New Guard

which he did with real enthusiasm. The storage area was now a battlefield, with grenades flying through the air and the sound of shots from panic stricken troops. "Keep pushing forward" Dutch screamed at Bentley as they inched closer to their goal.

Rommel was ordering and screaming at the troops to move forward, that the operatives must be caught.

Dr Einer Stiener, Maximilian and Fredrick in tow were making their way to the storage area when the explosions started. "What? Fools if that collar becomes damaged there will be hell to pay!" The Dr announced. With that Maximilian rushed off in the direction of the explosions to help his brother to succeed in the mission. The Dr and Fredrick carried on at a leisurely pace. The Dr turned to Fredrick

CASE FILE:- The New Guard

then sinisterly said "Take your time, only the fool's rush towards their death...." Fredrick gulped at the thought of all those lives being lost as they casually walked towards the fire fight.

Dutch and Bentley were almost at the trench wall, when all of a sudden a charge of figures came leaping down in to the trench. In the confusion and smoke Dutch couldn't make out who they were? He thought to himself we're done for now! But a voice sung out "This way lads lets push the Germans back!" They were British Human troops, British troops Dutch acknowledged, but their running in to a trap! Without a further thought for his own safety he dropped everything in his paws and

CASE FILE:- The New Guard

sprinted towards the British troops. Just as the first officer was to turn a stack of crates and enter in to a hail of bullets he was struck in the stomach by a small black and tan terrier pushing him back. Dutch felt the heat and wind of something that had hit him as he flew through the air as he intercepted the officer. Dutch lay on top of him and he caught the smell of burning hair. He couldn't feel anything then slowly turned his head to check his body and there was the tip of his tail singed where a bullet had passed. The human officer looked at him as Dutch laid on his chest saw the damage to Dutch's tail and just said "you're one lucky lad!" Dutch licked his face and collapsed with exhaustion. The officer moved Dutch out of

CASE FILE:- The New Guard

harms reach and then assessed the situation. The battle was still in full swing and Bentley was now in the middle of it, all on his own.

A human corporal positioned himself next to the officer and asked what they were to do next? As the corporal stood there he could see through the smoke a small chubby Bulldogge doing his best to stand his ground with grenades being thrown this way and that. As he watched the scene in front of him, it brought back memories of his own two dogs and his Bulldogge Bentley back home. He hadn't seen Dutch as he had been at the end of the line as they had gone across the battlefield, so initially it didn't sink in that these two heroes could be his boys.

CASE FILE:- The New Guard

Bentley was down to his last two grenades and the troops were drawing in closer and closer, every time he tried to make a move towards the British troops

sniper fire would pin him down. He was scared and felt so alone, he didn't know what had happened to his friend so feared the worst.

As the Corporal and The Officer stood there almost helpless to be able to do anything a soldier came forward and announced "He's awake Sir and he's trying to get back in to the battle!" The Corporal looked at him puzzled and just behind the soldier being held firmly for his own good was Dutch. In an instant Dutch and Kevin recognised each other.

CASE FILE:- The New Guard

"Soldier let him go!" Kevin ordered. Dutch rushed forward to greet his master, his friend. Kevin bent down and hugged him for all he was worth. "What in the hell or you doing here lad?" Kevin questioned. But before that question could be answered it suddenly dawned on him that that was Bentley who was in trouble!

Kevin turned to Dutch and ordered him "Stay here!" Kevin moved to the front of the crates and looked at the officer. The officer could sense what the corporal was going to do next. "Don't do it, it's only a dog!" he said. Kevin looked him in the eyes and replied "he's not just a dog, he family, he's my

CASE FILE:- The New Guard

boy." As he started to sprint towards Bentleys position.

As Kevin ran towards Bentley's position the bullets were ripping past him with every step and everything seemed to be in slow motion. A sniper was just positioning himself with a bead on Bentley!

Kevin knew what he had to do, with one last bit of effort he threw himself at Bentley and knocked him off of his feet. Kevin felt a burning sensation then pain; he had been shot!

Bentley didn't know what was happening? In the confusion someone had flattened him, so he quickly reacted defensively by growling and snapping.

CASE FILE:- The New Guard

Kevin looked up and murmured "It's me boy, it's me." Bentley lent down and sniffed. It was Kevin! He was relieved to see his master and started to lick his face. But was confused that Kevin was not reacting? He looked down Kevin's body and could see the bloody uniform.

Dutch at this time had moved to a better position to see what was happening, but yet again he was being held back for his own good. Dutch screamed and howled at the sight in front of him as it looked that all hope was lost.

Bentley looked at Kevin and back towards the British troops, he knew what he had to do. Summing up all his courage he gripped hold of Kevin's

CASE FILE:- The New Guard

jacket and started to pull him towards safety. Bentley pulled and pulled, slowly inching Kevin to safety with each step. A Bullet just passed his head, he dropped to floor for second then carried on.

The British troops could see Bentleys efforts and were willing him on and trying their best to reach him as they eased out in to the fire fight. It was only when a soldier patted Bentley on the head and said "Don't worry pup, we've got him now." That Bentley knew he had made it. The human soldiers pulled Kevin away under fire to a safe position as Bentley followed.

CASE FILE:- The New Guard

Medics were called for Kevin who was taken away. Bentley stood there shaking trying to take in what had just happened, when a familiar paw touched him on the shoulder, as he turned to see who it was. Dutch moved in and gave him a hug. "My old friend I'm so proud of you." Bentley relieved to see him, picked Dutch up and swung him about in hug of joy.

"Fall back!" Came a command from the officer. The human soldiers started to make their way back to their own lines across no man's land.

"Come on you two!" a soldier said in passing to our two heroes. Bentley let go of Dutch and turned to move back with the troops. Dutch stood there a second, looking at Bentley. The penny dropped.

CASE FILE:- The New Guard

"Bentley where's the time collar?" Dutch asked. "I don't know, I thought you had it?" He replied. "OH NO!" Dutch yelled.

Dutch moved to see the area where they had been, it was now covered in enemy troops with General Rommel in the midst of them all. Rommel bent down, picked up the time collar then dusted it off. He turned a glance towards Dutch's position he smiled then turned and walked away. Dutch was panicking, but before he could make a decision he was detained by two British soldiers for his own good, and then taken back to British lines.

As they crossed no man's land the repeating thoughts haunted Dutch, We failed our mission, we failed, as he hung his head low.

CASE FILE:- The New Guard

Chapter 13 .... You can always find success from failure.

As Dutch and Bentley stood waiting to hear on the results of Kevin's injury outside the field hospital, the discussion was sullen to do with the loss of the time collar and Kevin's injury. It had been a week since their rescue even though Kevin had survive

they had no idea what the result of the injury would do for his future?

A nurse came through the doors and asked "Are you Kevin's friends?" "Yes Miss." Dutch replied.

CASE FILE:- The New Guard

"You can see him now." she answered. The pair followed the nurse to where Kevin was resting.

Around Kevin's bed stood a group of people in discussion. Dutch made his excuses and pushed through the group with Bentley following close behind. Kevin was discussing something with a Human General and looked pretty glum.

"I'm sorry corporal but due to your injury to your hip the Army can no longer have you in active service." The General told him. "But Sir, I'm sure I will heal!" Kevin replied. The General looked at him then said "No, no. You've done your part. Time to go home and put your feet up, the war is over for you, son."

CASE FILE:- The New Guard

Dutch moved forward and laid his paw on the back of Kevin's hand. Kevin turned to see his boy's faces and realised what was most important. "If you say so Sir." he said to the General.

With that the crowd started to move away from his bed leaving initially Kevin and his two boys. Bentley moved around to Kevin's other hand to receive a stroke. "I know lads. What I still can't fathom out is what you two were doing there in the first place?" Before either Bentley or Dutch could speak a small voice spoke up as they walked towards Kevin's bed. Dutch and Bentley instantly recognised the voice. "Sir." Dutch acknowledged as brought himself and Bentley to attention then saluted.

CASE FILE:- The New Guard

Kevin sat there amazed at what was happening. There at the end of his bed was a small red Lakeland terrier with a magnificent moustache! Beside him was an English Bullterrier carrying a briefcase.

Dutch spoke up "I'm sorry sir, we failed our mission." The Brigadier replied "Don't worry I've read your report." "What Mission? Reports? What's going on and who are you?" Kevin questioned. "Sergeant Rosa could you, the Major and the Captain step outside for a moment I need a few minutes with the Corporal please." The Brigadier ordered. The three left then waited outside which gave the three of them time to catch up on their exploits.

CASE FILE:- The New Guard

The Brigadier sat on the edge of Kevin's bed then disclosed what his two boys had been doing and the mission they had been on. Once he had finished he asked a nurse to fetch the three back in. The three approached Kevin's bed, took one look at them and was overcome with emotion as tried hard to hold back the tears of pride he had for the pair of them.

"Now going back to your Mission" the Brigadier announced. "I know Sir, we're sorry about that." Dutch interrupted. "Let me finish please Major!" The Brigadier replied. "Sorry Sir." he answered. The Brigadier carried on "Right where was I? Oh yes the mission. Yes you failed. But under the

CASE FILE:- The New Guard

circumstances I couldn't be more proud of you if I tried."

Dutch looked at Bentley; Bentley looked at Dutch in shock! "Why sir?" Bentley asked. The Brigadier replied "Yes you didn't retrieve the time collar, but you stuck to the core of the S.D.S values." "Sir?" Bentley questioned still none the wiser. "You were willing to sacrifice your lives to save mankind." "So due to this true show of courage in the face of danger you have both been awarded these." Sergeant Rosa opened her brief case and laid it on the bed. Inside were two shining Dickin Medals for bravery. Kevin looked on with pride as his two boys received their medals.

CASE FILE:- The New Guard

"I'm not finished." The Brigadier carried on. He turned towards Kevin. "Corporal, I have read your reports and have spoken to your General." "Sir?" Kevin replied. The Brigadier said "I have been told that your military service is over." Kevin's face sank after being reminded of the fact. He answered slowly "Yes sir." "Hmm, well that means you'll have plenty of free time then? The Brigadier asked. "Yes sir." he replied. The Brigadier stopped then lent forward to the contents inside the briefcase on the bed. He then slowly said "Corporal, due to your Courage and sacrifice in the face of danger in saving not only a canine but a Watch dog Operative, I am awarding you the first of its kind. You Kevin are now an honouree member of the S.D.S, Watch Dog

CASE FILE:- The New Guard

Division!" The Brigadier then brought out of the briefcase a new ID wallet with Kevin's photo and HONOUREE OPERATIVE emblazed at the top. Kevin was shocked and embarrassed, "But sir, I just done what I had to do to save my boys." he said. The Brigadier looked him in the eyes then replied "That's why you deserve it. You have shown the same unselfish spirit as if you were a canine, so you're one of us now!" he smiled. "Thank you sir, I'm honoured." Kevin replied, then asked, "So what will I do?" The Brigadier answered "Because of your injury, you will help Colonel Butterriss in the Library." "The Library?"

CASE FILE:- The New Guard

Kevin asked. "Don't worry it will become clear when we return to base."

Dutch still worried, broke up the celebrations, by mentioning the time collar. The brigadier replied "Don't worry Colonel Butteriss is keeping an eye on the time lines as we speak, if there's a change we will deal with it." he carried on. "So let us get on our way to London. Kevin are you fit to travel?" "Not yet sir it will be a couple of more days yet." He replied.

The brigadier replied "Okay as soon as your fit, you'll travel with myself and Sergeant Rosa to London." "Yes Sir." Kevin answered. The Brigadier

CASE FILE:- The New Guard

then turned to Dutch and Bentley and told them to make their way to London immediately.

Dutch was about to say goodbye to Rosa but the Brigadier intervened and spoke up, "Before you go a couple of things. First of all due to this historic event of our new Honouree Operative I think Photos are called for and secondly Bentley there is something waiting for you behind that tent over there."

Before Bentley rushed off to find out what was behind the tent, Kevin had made his way out of the field hospital and had photos with the pair of his boys.

CASE FILE:- The New Guard

S.D.S Intelligence Report Photos.

The new Honouree Watch Dog Operative Kevin with Major Dude and Captain Poopstacker.

"Can I go and have a look now?" said an inpatient Bentley. "Yes go ahead." The Brigadier replied. Bentley rushed off behind the tent, and then suddenly there was a squeal of excitement. The next thing they heard an engine start and a POOP,

CASE FILE:- The New Guard

POOP! Yes Bentley was reunited with his beloved Morgan. Dutch smiled to himself at the outcome of their adventure, but was still worried what lay ahead for the future.

"Come on you two get going!" The Brigadier ordered. Dutch said his goodbyes to Rosa and hugged Kevin. "Take care and look after your little brother." Kevin quietly said in to Dutch's ear. Dutch replied "Of course as always.""I know." Kevin agreed. Dutch loaded his gear in to the Morgan whilst Bentley ran across to say goodbye to Kevin. Kevin hugged him and told him to be good lad and that he was proud of him. Bentley pretended to

CASE FILE:- The New Guard

adjust his monocle and wiped away a tear from his cheek, then said goodbye.

The Morgan roared off and with a POOP,POOP they were off on their way to London.

The Brigadier and Rosa were chatting with Kevin when a soldier appeared by side them carrying a telegram. The soldier gave the Brigadier the telegram and he opened it to read the message.

CASE FILE:- The New Guard

URGENT. RETURN TO BASE. TIME LINES.

LONDON AND THE EMPIRE IN PERIL.

COLONEL M BUTTERISS.

END OF REPORT.

CASE FILE:- The New Guard

Map of Europe 1915.

CASE FILE:- The New Guard

Map of Mission Objectives.